Vengeance

- punishment inflicted in retaliation for an injury or offense...

ALSO AVAILABLE

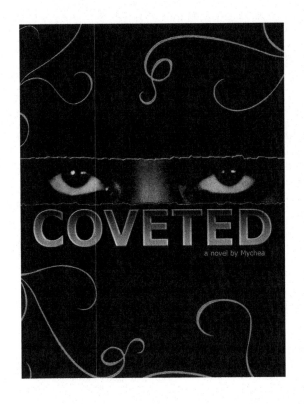

VENGEANCE

Mychea

www.mycheawrites.com

Copyright © 2010 by Mychea

All works are original works of Mychea.

ISBN: 1456346601

Cover Design: Michele Lee

Cover Photography: Rashad Nobles

Cover Make-Up: Marcy Patrick

Cover Models:

Brittany Robinson,

Sharee "Honey" Brown,

Leah Semiken

Tiffany Banks

Printed in the United States of America

This novel is dedicated to my biggest fan and personal cheerleader, my mom Cheryl Lee.
I love you.

Special Thanks

Much love to fellow author Silk White. Thank you for being a great mentor, a wonderful friend, an inspiration to me on a daily base and someone who knows enough about this crazy literary business to help me out. You have no idea how your words of wisdom have helped me through many of my unsure moments and how my vision has grown since meeting you, for that I am so grateful. You're an amazing writer whose opinion I value and respect and I truly thank you from the bottom of my heart just for being you.

~M~

Acknowledgments

You guys!!! This is my second novel! Pretty cool right!?! First, I must thank God for giving me the gift of creative writing. I love that I was chosen for this sort of entertainment.

To my parents, Thomas and Cheryl Lee, thanks for being able to raise a creative child such as myself...had to be rough, but look at me now! :0)

Sending a shout out to my older siblings, Thomas and Syreeta Lee thanks for looking out for your little sis.

Marcy Patrick, thank you for being there. I don't know how I would sell books, book signings, make appearances and just be, without you. I truly am grateful for you being on the Mychea Writes team; because of you I am that much better. The million dollar dream continues.

Tara Moore, thank you for being another asset to the Mychea Writes team. The business mind that keeps the force together.... cause girlie, I'm pure artist, thanks for helping a shortie out. Thanks for everything you have done and continue to do and for being a great friend!

Nikki Jackson, thank you for being the best editor ever! The editor with the mostest!!! (Hahahaha don't get mad, I know mostest isn't a word. LOL!). I also want to thank you for being a fabulous individual. You may not be a blood sister, but you're the next best thing. You Rock!!!

Mia Wallace, we go back to long walks home from elementary school, to chilling on the corner after long bus rides from Middle and High School. Will never forget and will cherish those moments forever. I can truly say you are the one person in the whole world that understands me the most and I wouldn't trade my number one road dog for the world.

Me'Shell Stewart and Tandace Wilson we all go way, way, way back. Thank you both for keeping me sane as my schedule gets more and more hectic. I love the normalcy you bring to my life. Love you guys.

Judy Bowens, thank you for taking the time out your day to prepare such a great meal when Coveted first hit the streets and inviting people over to meet me and purchase my novel. I am truly thankful for your support.

Courtney Jones, Marcie Rodriguez, Princess Rodriguez, Tracey Young, Marlene Saez, Nana Morales, Sonya Coleman, Roxie Stennett, Katrina Monroe, Derrick Brown, Josephine Thomas, Phyllis "My Phyllis" Williams, Sean Plater and Barbara Wright, I thank each of you for being a part of my life and for sharing your awesome personalities with me.

Special thank you to a few more of my cousins for the joy and laughter they bring to my life, Kesha Carroll, Belinda (Tweety) Carroll, LaShawn Bomen, LaWan White, Tekeema Bowens, and Sabrina Carroll.

Model shout out time lol! Brittany Robinson, thanks for gracing the front of my cover. You look hot and the cover rocks! Sharee "Honey" Brown, thank you for gracing the cover of Coveted and also Vengeance. You are an awesome model and you always get it done! LOL! Leah Semiken, one of the people that I have known the longest in the world, lol, thank you for taking the time out to be a part of the Vengeance cover. Tiffany Ryan Banks, I also want to thank you for not doing one, but two photo shoots for Vengeance. Thanks for being there when I needed you. You're the best Lil Sis ever.

Tra Verdejo, Chrisopher Bell, Sr. and The Literary Joint Bookstore, I thank all of you for allowing me into your space to share my book with the world.

Special shout out to my fans Brian Christian, Leandra Baker, Princess Bridges and Carmen Thompson, who take time out of their day to hit me up on Facebook, Myspace, Twitter, LinkedIn, Tagged and my website.

To everyone that has left a review on Amazon or my Facebook page, thanks a million.

Thank you to all you readers, for taking time out your day to allow me to share my characters in your lives for a number of hours. That means the world to me and I hope you continue to enjoy the crazy journeys I love to take your minds on. Thank you all for keeping my dream alive. I am grateful to you forever.

Email: mychea@mycheawrites.com
Website: www.mycheawrites.com

My heart stopped beating
EMOTIONALLY

The hurt consumes me
Darkness won't let me go
BE STILL

My mind keeps the secrets locked
HELP ME

Don't watch me sink
As I go lower
Screaming silently
You think everything is fine
IT'S NOT

My eyes hold many untold stories
Nightmares Even
You couldn't even begin to imagine

You see me and see what I want you to see
You don't even know me
Can't you tell the difference in your friend?
I can always tell differences in you

Observing everything
Seeing all
Not as attentive as me
They assume they know me
They'll see
No one knows me
Not even me

PAY ATTENTION
Hear what I don't say
Look beyond the smile
Remember eyes tell all

See me
I'm not perfect
I'M NOT PERFECT!

My heart hurts
My mind runs sideways
I'm on the edge
About to fall off
No one notices
I'm about to fall

One look back
A silent plea
One step forward
I FALL
They didn't see me

Screams, Shouts
Oh, now they want to notice
Too late
You noticed too late

I screamed silently
Why couldn't you hear me?
My eyes told every story
Why didn't you listen to me?

So many tears
It looks like heartache
All who didn't appreciate
Now trying to perpetrate

They said
I was larger than life
So much energy and love
What do they know?

Oh! Wait there's more
Loved by all
What a lie
If loved by all
Why didn't anyone say
Goodbye?

-Namiyah

Prologue

Pressed against the wall, gasping for air as his fingers tightened around my throat, my mind wanted to take a leave of absence. I knew if I stopped concentrating on breathing and passed out, this would mark the end of my existence, right here at this spot, in this dirty alley and I refused to have the story of my life end this way. Frantically reaching my hands into the back pocket of my jeans as he continued to squeeze the air from my body, I knew I didn't have much longer before consciousness was lost. Finally, feeling what I was searching for, I made my move quickly. With the blade concealed in my hand, I raised my arm up and dug the tip into the back of his neck with all my might. Yelling in pain, he released one hand from around my throat, to grab the back of his neck, giving me a second to suck air back into my deprived lungs. A second is all the time I needed. Not giving him a chance to continue the assault, I raised the blade masked in my hand, and cut the wrist that was co-conspirator to the hand that was trying, though unsuccessfully now, to cut off my air supply.

With him now withering in pain, it was amusing to see the assaulter now become the assaulted. Table turned, taking full advantage of the situation, I was not letting him get away with what he did to me. Blade swinging, I got him to the ground. Straddling him, I proceeded to keep slicing. He moved his hands to cover his face. Little did he know I didn't want his face; I wanted his throat, which was exposed. Walking away from the stilled body, I grinned from ear to ear, my smile mirroring the deep gash the police would find etched in his throat.

Chapter 1

Vowing that she would have her revenge, Camille shook her head as she thought about the years of waiting for both of them. Now the time was right and neither were making good on promises that had been made.

Sitting at her computer, it was going to take some doing, but she would find all the information she needed. She hadn't spent her last two years of college working as a receptionist under Naima at Exclusively Divine Events for no reason. She was the best internet researcher out there by far. Smiling to herself, "Yeah I'm definitely the best and changes need to be made."

Frowning as the phone rang, interrupting her thoughts, she reached for the receiver.

"Camille, I need to see you."

Giving the phone an exasperated sigh, Camille fought to keep the indifference out of her voice.

"What's the matter Chris?"

"Haven, is acting like a lunatic. Going through my phone and checking my messages. She swears I'm cheating on her."

Taking in a slow breath, Camille couldn't believe his audacity.

"But you are cheating on her."

"Camille, baby what am I supposed to do?"

Closing her eyes, she thought, "How did I ever get myself into this stupid situation? Chris is a mess and I am a mess right along with him for going along with this foolishness."

"How am I to know what you are supposed to do with your wife?" Shaking her head; walking over to the mirror, Camille stared at her reflection. She noticed the bags under her eyes due to lack of sleep. Living a double life was definitely taking its toll.

"What would you suggest?"

I would suggest that you keep your promises to me, she thought to herself, but instead verbalized, "Chris, I don't know. I've never been married and don't have a pregnant wife, so I'm not sure what you should do."

"I thought you would be the one person that could understand and not give me attitude."

Camille could feel her blood rising to its boiling point, "Why, because I'm white? Don't get it backwards honey, we don't like to be done wrong either and we have attitudes too." The nerve of him, white women aren't all that different from black women. He was more than welcome to try her and see.

"Hey, that's not what I meant and you know it." Chris said trying his best to defend himself. But she had his ass and he knew it. He had assumed he wouldn't have to deal with as much attitude from her, but he'd be damned if he let her know it.

Grunting in disbelief, "Good," she said.

Bidding his time wisely, Chris was waiting for the perfect opportunity to set his plan into motion. If he had learned nothing else in jail, he had learned patience. That was something that he could definitely be credited with. These last couple of years had been bittersweet, because he knew that inevitably, all good things must come to an end and the end was in sight.

"Hey baby, what you up to in here?"

Looking up as Haven was coming into the room; Chris had to admit she looked pretty, her swollen belly entering the room before she did. Leaning down to kiss him softly on the forehead she went over to sit in the recliner.

Chris pushed his notes aside so that he could focus his attention on her, "Just going over some work. How are you feeling?"

"I'm ok." She answered, raising her hand to rub her stomach, "This baby seems to be really angry with me about something. Feels like he or she has declared war inside of me." Closing her eyes as she leaned her head back, "I don't remember it being this difficult to carry Kaven."

"You have to remember that you were a lot younger when you had Kaven. It's been twelve years since then. Your body is probably wondering why you are doing this to it again after all this time."

She sighed, "Maybe you're right, a significant amount of time has passed since the last time I was pregnant."

"You should rest more," Chris said genuinely concerned.

Rotating her neck slowly from one side to the next, "Ugh, I have to work and I still want to be at all of Kaven's football games. I'm his biggest fan; I have to support my baby." Exhaling a tired sigh, "I don't foresee rest in my future."

"I understand that, but you really need to chill out more. Something happen to my baby, you and I are going to have some serious issues."

Haven felt a chill go down her spine. It wasn't Chris' words; it was the way he said it. Maybe that was the reason this pregnancy was so difficult. Her spirit was uneasy. She had an eerie feeling that something bad was going to take place and much sooner than later.

Ever since Amber had been killed, she had been trying to get her life in order. Amber's death made everything hit home for her. Realizing how precious life is and how no moment should be taken for granted; she had went above and beyond to make amends with Naima, which had been no easy task. But having your childhood friend fighting for her life tends to put things into perspective very quickly. Haven had spent as much time at the hospital as humanly possible, which also afforded her and Kaden the opportunity to call a truce. She had paid all the money she owed him out right, with Chris' help of course. She still didn't believe that Kaden was very fond of her, but hey, that was another battle to overcome at another time. She was just thankful that he had helped with the process of Naima forgiving her. She would owe him for the rest of his life for that deed alone.

Kaden was the one who had told Naima that Haven had spent countless hours at the hospital while she was in the Intensive Care Unit. Lots of counseling sessions and tears later, she and Naima were finally in a good place. It wasn't a perfect place, but they were mending and healing their relationship slowly. Day by day their friendship was definitely getting stronger.

"Chris, you know I would never do anything to intentionally hurt our baby."

Chris was now bored with this conversation. Rising to his feet he walked over and kissed her on the forehead. "I know you wouldn't. I have to go into the office for a couple of hours; will you be ok while I am gone?"

Haven waved him off, "I'll be fine. Kaven should be getting dropped off soon, so you need not worry," she smiled up at him, "I'm good."

"Cool." He couldn't move quick enough to get out the house. Sometimes his intense hatred for Haven over took him and he could no longer keep up the lie. She was irrelevant in his world. He was dealing with Haven like a game of chess. Everything was about strategic movement.

The baby would be here soon, that was the only thing that he was thrilled about. Haven's getting pregnant had been an unexpected turn of events, but now that she was carrying another one of his children, he would have to delay his plan for a little longer. He wasn't worried about that, however, it was inevitable and Haven's time would come.

Parking his car in front of his destination, Chris was already aroused. Only Camille had the power to do this to him. At twenty-six there was a freshness about her that was hard to find in the thirty and over women his age. Camille added the extra spice that he needed in his life.

He'd met Camille almost six years ago. He had begun to take some grad classes at the University of Maryland and she had been working on her undergraduate degree in Finance. It was a crazy twist of fate that Camille worked for Naima and through that connect he had been able to find Haven. After being released from jail, he moved back to the Metropolitan area solely for that purpose alone.

Camille had left the door cracked open for him and when Chris walked in, he could already smell the aroma of chicken frying. Momentarily forgetting about his arousal, mouth already watering, he headed toward the salivating smell. He smiled as he walked in and saw Camille standing over the stove with her Betty Boop apron on.

Camille was above average in the looks department. Standing at five – two, one hundred and twenty pounds, she was very tiny. With her auburn hair, milky white skin and freckles that lightly sprinkled over her nose, she reminded Chris of Lucille Ball from "I Love Lucy". One of the bonuses to Camille was that she could throw down in the kitchen and one of her specialties was soul food. Chris used to marvel at black women that couldn't boil water, let alone cook soul food. If Camille could get it done and get it done well, why couldn't they?

Walking up behind Camille, he placed his hands around her waist. "Hey Babe," he said as he leaned down and gently kissed her neck. Turning in his arms to face him, Camille rose on her tippy toes to kiss him fully on the mouth. Chris received her kiss and bent over to scoop her up in his arms.

Laughing as she broke the kiss off, "Hey put me down, I have to finish cooking. You don't want to eat charred chicken do you?"

"Baby, I would still eat it because you cooked it for me. Now let's go handle my other hunger first. The apron is cute, but I want it off." Chris was already feeling up under her apron trying to unbuckle her jeans so he could feel her skin.

"Chris stop." She said, swatting his hand away from her jeans still laughing, "I am not burning down my kitchen fooling with you. Now put me down please."

Chris finally obliged, but not without coping an extra feel first. "Ok, ok, you win." Returning her feet to the floor, "I'll leave you be," pulling her close to him so she could feel the full length of him, "for now."

"Thank you, I appreciate it Mr. Impatient." Making her way back over to the stove to check on the chicken, Camille glanced back at Chris, "If you need something to occupy your time, you can chop those vegetables over on the table for me."

Smiling slightly, "I've only been here a few minutes and you already trying to put me to work?"

"Yup, you know it. You know where the knives are," she gestured toward the counter drawers, "help yourself."

Walking over to the counter to pull a knife, Chris went to the table and started slicing vegetables.

"How is Haven's pregnancy coming along?"

Damn, Chris thought. I'm really not in the mood to discuss Haven. But Camille had proven her loyalty and been a good sport about him marrying Haven and now with the new baby on the way, the least he could do was be honest with her and answer all of her questions.

Taking in a slow easy breath, he responded, "This one seems to be giving her difficulties. She's really having a rough time."

"Oh," she said speaking softly, "are you excited about the baby?"

Putting the knife down, walking back up to her, "I'm excited about you." Chris said, scooping Camille up into his arms again. Reaching over to cut off the stove, "Dinner can wait, me making love to you cannot."

Giggling softly, Camille offered no resistance this time. "Well ok, Mr. Impatient, but don't be trying to get over on me. I still expect my after dinner dessert."

"Don't worry; I will have plenty left over for dessert later."

An hour and a half later Camille was scurrying around the kitchen in nothing but her Betty Boop apron, cleaning up the remains of the dinner they had just finished eating.

"Are you staying over tonight?"

"Do you want me to?"

"Chris you know I always want you here. When are you going to be done with this thing with Haven?" There was tiredness in Camille's tone. Chris could tell that the Haven situation was beginning to take a toll on her.

Groaning inwardly Chris knew that this conversation was coming sooner than later. He just thought that she would give him more time and it would happen later.

"I'm not sure yet. The baby has pushed things back a little."

Camille was seething mad. She hated anything that had to do with Haven or the baby for that matter. She still remembered her last encounter with Haven.

Why is it that black women come with so much drama? If I knew the answer to that question I would be a freakin' millionaire instead of working for wacko Mrs. Fairchild. I swear sometimes I don't think that she has it all there. She is loony as hell. Always trying to act high and mighty like her life is peaches and cream. Well it sure went up in smoke right in front of her face did it not?

Ms. Haven is funny, crazy as all hell, but funny. It was hilarious to see her sashay her way in here to start some mess and end up slam on her ass. I didn't mean to eavesdrop, okay, maybe I did. But it was funny and all I did was asked her if she needed tissue for her bloody face, she didn't have to ignore me. I'm not the one that slapped her. Best entertainment that I have seen in a long time and I am in the modeling industry, well kind of. I mean, I model in fashion shows, one day someone will wake up and notice my talent.

I am in my last couple of days at school at the University of Maryland. One more final to go and college life will be over, thank goodness. I'm about ready to be done. It has taken me five long years to prove to everyone that I have what it takes to make it, not just another pretty face. Once I get my degree I can get a new job. Exclusively Divine Events does not pay me enough to put up with Naima's mess. She obviously has a miserable life and I think she gets joy out of making my life a living hell. Every once in a while she has a good day; I look forward to those. I mean I don't hate her or anything and I think it's really jacked up that her best friend was sexing her man and had the nerve to have a baby by him. That is so foul and Mrs. Fairchild is a good one because I would have cut that hoe, plain and simple. But just because she is miserable does she have to take her crap out on me? I have enough on my plate; I have finals, and this job, ugh, the tragedy.

Usually Camille kept her feelings to herself, but Haven was a skank as far as she was concerned. Any woman that would sleep with her best friend's husband could not be trusted. Chris seemed content with dragging this situation out, but Camille was not having it.

"You should be using protection with her anyway. If you had been, there would be no baby and my life wouldn't still be on hold."

Chris looked at Camille incredulously, "How would I explain using protection with my own wife? Haven ain't going for that."

"Baby, but what about me," Camille pouted, "How long do you expect me to wait?"

Sitting down in a chair and pulling her into his lap, Chris pushed her hair back so he could caress the side of her face.

"Camille, you have been a great sport about this whole thing. Trust me; it won't last too much longer. Just let my baby get here and then the countdown can begin."

Standing, turning to look down at him, "I'm giving you one year and then I'm gone. I've been waiting patiently for over five years. I'm missing my life, waiting on you to live yours and I'm done with this." Looking him dead in his eyes so that he knew she was serious, she repeated for emphasis, "One year."

Seeing the sadness and anger in her eyes, Chris knew that she meant it, there was only a matter of time before she left him and he couldn't really be mad at her, she was tired of the games. Running his hand over his face, he had to act and he had to act fast. Camille had made it very clear, he had one year. Let the new countdown begin.

Turning the television off in the family room, Haven looked up at the clock hanging above the fireplace. It was well after two in the morning. "Where in the hell is Chris?" she thought to herself. Kaven had been home, eaten dinner and was now in bed and yet, still there was no sign of Chris. "There is no way that he is still in the office," she said out loud to the silence or God if he was listening. Haven dialed his cell one more time; once again, all she received was his voicemail. Chris was up to something. This wasn't the first time he's stayed out late or not come home at all.

Still clutching the phone, Haven called Naima, she was so grateful to have Naima back in her life.

"Hello." A sleepy voice answered.

"Hey Nai."

"Hey," clearing her throat, Haven could hear her shifting on the phone, "Oh-oh, what's wrong? Chris M-I-A again?"

Closing her eyes and leaning her head against the phone, "I can't believe I put this friendship in jeopardy, no one knows me like Naima." Haven said to herself.

"Girl, how did you guess?"

"Why else would you be calling me after two in the morning? If your man was home, you wouldn't be thinking about me."

"Very true. I just don't know what's up with him. Something is not sitting right with me about our whole situation."

"Well what's wrong?" Naima sounded more alert now, "Do you think he's cheating on you?"

Haven took a deep breath, slowly releasing it from her lips.

"I don't know. I just have a feeling that he's up to something. You know?"

"Well, doesn't he work long hours anyway? Maybe he's still working." Naima knew that there may very well be a strong possibility that Chris was cheating on Haven. He was showing all of the classic signs, not returning phone calls, not coming home at night, or if he did bother to come, he came very late and offered no explanations. Naima didn't want to have an "I told you so moment" but Karma can be a real "B". Haven had done so many foul things in her life that there was bound to be something that would come back and bite her in the ass.

"Yeah, he does work long hours. But sometimes I feel as if

he uses his job as a cover up."

"Haven, worrying about this will drive you crazy. At eight months pregnant, you really don't need this stress right now. If Chris says he's working then until you have proof that he isn't, let it go. Trust me," Naima continued, "it's so much better for your sanity that way."

Haven thought about what Naima was saying for a second. She hated to admit it, but Naima did make sense, but she wasn't buying it. Chris was definitely up to something and if anyone should understand, Naima should. Seeing as she would not be making any head way tonight, Haven decided to drop the subject.

"I guess you're right. I don't want to stress and mess around and go into labor early about something I can't do anything about right now anyway."

"Good for you." Naima said, yawning over the phone, "Get some rest. If things keep going as they're going, don't worry, what's done in the dark will come to light eventually."

"Aight girl, thanks for listening. I really needed to vent."

"Haven, I'm always here for you, only a phone call away."

Hanging up the phone, Haven still had an unsettling feeling, but in all actuality, what could she do with no proof? Maybe it was best to take Naima's advice, Chris couldn't cover up whatever he was doing for long, and eventually everything would come out into the open.

Chapter 2

Interlude

Squeezing her eyes shut, Emeri wanted to yell out so badly. It took everything in her to concentrate on not screaming. There is no way she could ever tell her Mama, she wouldn't know what to do. Emeri felt as if she went through so much already. This would break her and she didn't want anything bad happening to her. He had told Emeri if she ever said a word that he would kill her. There was no way Emeri could let that happen, nothing bad could ever happen to her mother, she's all Emeri has in the world. Without her, there is nothing.

I knew he would be back for more. He always came back. He acts as if he can't stay away from me. I feel caged. I do everything I can to remain normal and do what is required of me, but inside I am dying. My soul is aching, why can no one see what he is doing to me? He's slowly killing me. My spirit is tormented.

Men are all the same. Always wanting what they want, never

thinking or caring about anyone's feelings but their own in return. He would not continue this assault on me forever. One of these days, he is going to pay. I don't know how, but it is coming and much sooner than later.
I have had enough.

The sooner Emeri could get out of this fuckin' place the better. "I swear," she thought, "if I have to be housed in here with all these crazies another minute, I really will be able to be categorized as one of them. I'm just over this whole experience." The judge had sentenced her to five years in the psych ward of the prison. She was set to be discharged the following morning and it couldn't come soon enough. Who knew, there really was a God. Cause Lord knows, if she had to talk to Coleen one more time, she was going to lose it. For the life of her, she couldn't understand why Coleen was chosen as her therapist. It's as if they knew that jail in the psych ward wasn't enough, she had to be punished even further. Well they had succeeded. Emeri didn't think it could get any worse than Coleen. The court system had the nerve to say, that she had to report to Coleen until they felt she was no longer a threat to society. If anything, Coleen's ass was a threat to them in here.

Kenneth was on his way for their weekly Thursday therapy session, ever since Emeri had been put in there, this had become their routine. She thought that he was trying to forgive her, trying to get to a point where the two of them could have a relationship. They had been doing these sessions so long; Emeri had come to love and loath them. On the one hand, she was happy that she finally was getting a chance to know my dad after all of these years; all she ever wanted to have was a Dad. She believed the sessions had actually brought them closer together. On the other hand, she hated how they are trying to make everything seem like it was her fault. It was never her intention to hurt Naima. Emeri was hurt too; she lost her mother, someone she loved too. It wasn't her fault that Naima had jumped in front of the bullet marked with Damir's name on it. As far as Emeri was concerned, for the most part, they could all suck it.

Serves Damir right, now with Amber and Naima out the picture, maybe he could forgive Emeri for the birthday incident, she didn't think he would really stay angry with her forever? The sooner he could let go and let God, the sooner they could get their life in order. Emeri had heard about the birth of his baby girl on the night of his party. What an incredible way to enter the world. It's unfortunate that she lost her mom, but look at the plus side; she was here against all odds and in the midst of adversity.

Sighing deeply as she stood to go to therapy, Emeri glanced around her solitary padded, white room. She had been deemed unfit to have a roommate, which when she first arrived she had appreciated. Now though, she missed not having someone to talk to. With only Coleen and Kenneth to have any form of communication with the outside world, she was losing the little bit of mind they thought she had left. Smiling to herself, tomorrow they would definitely see a new her. She would finally be free of this place.

"So Emeri," Coleen began, raising her perfectly arched eyebrow at me. Already she was irking Emeri, speaking to her with the slow patient voice as if she were five. "How would you like for today's session to go?"

"I'm not sure what you mean." Emeri responded, leaning her

head to the side and staring at her. She knew exactly what Coleen meant, but she's the one with the PhD, let her figure Emeri out.

Shifting her notepad to her lap giving Emeri a dead on stare, "Emeri, don't you know that if you willingly participate in our sessions, I will be able to give the judge an accurate accounting of your behavioral changes and just maybe, you won't have to endure counseling with me any longer? The choice is yours." Rising from her chair next to Emeri, she went back and sat at her desk to go over paperwork, dismissing her as if she no longer existed.

Sighing indifferently, resigning to her fate, "What would you like to know?"

Raising her eyes above the papers she was reviewing, Coleen looked at Emeri long and hard before she spoke, "I am trying to help you. If you don't want my help, there's the door." Looking back down at her papers, she dismissed her again.

Narrowing her eyes and breathing heavily as she pressed her tongue to the back of her teeth,

Emeri wanted to bash Coleen's skull in. Coleen knew goodness well that she could not leave and that she had to see her in order to remain outside of jail. Who did she think that she was kidding?

"Coleen, if you are willing, I would like to proceed." Emeri said as graciously as she could muster through gritted teeth.

Dropping her papers completely down on the desk this time, Coleen rose from her chair grabbing her notepad and went to sit in the seat next to Emeri that she had vacated not too long ago.

"I'm glad that we are coming to an understanding. I am not the enemy, I know it may seem that way, but I really want to help you succeed, so that you will be able to regain your life and be able to move on." Coleen's imploring eyes stared at Emeri's, "Let me help you Emeri, I want to."

Emeri looked at Coleen as if she were an alien from another planet. Did this broad think that she was delusional? Coleen didn't want to help her. All she was concerned about was her paycheck and making herself look good. Counseling Emeri just offered her an opportunity to boast about turning a judge-an-jury-deemed "insane" person around. Emeri would not be a part of her bullshit.

"Coleen, let's be honest. This is just a job for you, no more no less. So please spare me the dramatics. All I want is to do my sessions and be done with this."

"Until I feel that we have made progress, you will continue with these sessions. They can take however long or short a period, as you would like them too. The decision is ultimately yours." Continuing her vocalization to herself, as far as Emeri was concerned, "A parole board already vouched on your behalf that you are able and ready to reenter society. These sessions are just to ensure that you stay there." Placing her notepad on her lap, "All I can do is offer my help, you are the one that has to make the difference."

"Ok, fine. Let's start."

Remaining silent a moment longer, she began, "Ok, how about we take some time to talk about the night that put you in here with us." Emeri could already feel her face getting hot as Coleen continued, "I think it is time that you and your sister have a talk. A significant amount of time has passed since the shooting; this will give you an opportunity to sit with Naima and deal with the situation head on, not just go off of what your father has been telling you." Raising that infamous eyebrow again, she continued, "I know part of you is curious to see her, if for no other reason than to appease your curiosity. This can begin the road of healing for both of you. What do you think?"

Slowly rubbing her temple, Emeri tried to hear Coleen out, but wasn't feeling her. "I think you're the crazy one and maybe I should be counseling you."

"Emeri, I've had enough." Snapping her neck to the side, Emeri was in shock, she couldn't believe that Kenneth had spoken to her in that terse tone of voice.

"Excuse me?"

Standing up so he could look down at her, "You heard me, I've had enough. You have taken leave of your senses for too long. It is time for us to get to the bottom of whatever issues you are having."

"No offense Kenneth," Emeri began while slowly rising to my feet, "but it's a little too late to be taking on the parental role. I managed just fine without you for the first twenty-four years of my life, what makes you think I need you now?"

"That's your problem. You want to prove to the world you don't need anyone, when it's so obvious that the need and want for someone is gradually killing you."

One thing Emeri did know was that Kenneth had better calm his ass down, talking to her as if he has lost his mind. It would do him good to remember who he was dealing with.

"Kenneth," she paused for emphasis, "Please stop this charade. The only person I ever needed was my Mama and she's no longer here. Don't be fooled, I don't need you or anyone."

Taking on a softer tone, "It is not my intent to come into your life and try and tell you what to do. But you have come into my life wrecking havoc since you first walked through my front door." Taking Emeri's face into his hands so that she had no choice but to look at him, "If I had known about you I would have been there every step of the way, I would have seen you graduate at the top of your class and been at all the school plays. I would have been there." Emeri could see the moisture building in his eyes, "In spite of what you think, I need you in my life. I need us to somehow, some way make our world right, a world that can include you, Naima, my wife and me. I long for that, even if you do not."

Averting her eyes from his, Emeri refused to cry. She'd be damned if she would let him get to her. She wasn't stupid by any means. She knew deep down that it wasn't his fault that he didn't get to see her grow up. She knew it was her Mama's fault, but unfortunately for everyone, her Mama wasn't around to blame and Emeri had to blame someone. Naima came to mind. She knew Kenneth wanted them to be one big happy family, but Naima would always be the one that was privileged to have what Emeri had longed for her whole life. Nothing could ever change that.

Nothing could change the fact that Kenneth was selfish enough to have an affair with a young girl and leave her high and dry once things worked out in his marriage. He had discarded her Mama as if she was a toy that he had outgrown. That is also a reality that cannot be changed and Emeri would never forget. The price for what he did would be paid.

Gently removing her face from his hands, "Kenneth, I don't know if that will ever happen. But if it will make you happy, I am more than willing to try."

His face lit up and his whole demeanor changed. That's when she saw it, the gleam in his kind eyes when they crinkled gently at the corner as he smiled.

"This is wonderful progress." Emeri rolled her eyes at the ceiling as Coleen began to speak. Ugh, just the sound of Coleen's voice annoyed her. "What the two of you have accomplished here today is great. I, however, would like to be in attendance when Emeri has her first meeting with Naima." Coleen turned to face Emeri, "Emeri, I want you to understand that for a while Naima may not want to be bothered with you. Considering what she has endured over the past few years because of something that is a direct result of what you did, can be overwhelming for her to deal with at first. All I ask is that you practice patience and not get discouraged."

Seriously, Coleen could have saved her breath and words for someone that gave a damn. As far as Emeri was concerned, Naima did not exist in her world. She would do what was necessary to appease Kenneth for the time being, until she could put some type of plan in motion.

Chapter 3

Looking up as Kaden and Kalani come through the door, Naima couldn't help smiling. Namiyah might have been a spitting image of her dad, but Kalani got it all from his Momma and at seven years old, he wasn't her little baby anymore. Eyes watering slightly, he was getting so big, so fast; too fast, she thought.

Seeing Naima sitting on the chaise in the family room with her favorite book "Coveted" open in her lap, Kalani dropped his book bag in the doorway and ran over to give her a hug. Closing her eyes Naima relished in the moment, thinking to herself, "I love being a mom."

"Hey big boy, how was your day today?"

Pulling out of the hug, Kalani went back to retrieve his bag. "It was great." He announced, face full of animation. Taking something out of his bag, he ran back over to Naima and practically shoved it in her face. Shifting so she could see what he was holding out to her without losing an eye in the process, she waited for him to continue speaking.

"We had arts and crafts today and I made this heart for you." Gently removing the red and white paper heart out of his hand, with "I love Mommy" written in crayon in the center, Naima melted. Reaching down and pulling him into another hug, she choked up. "I love this kid." She thought.

"Thank you punkin, I love it. I'm going to frame it and hang it on the wall." She said while reaching over to tap the tip of his nose, "If that's ok with you?"

Pulling away from her, he nods his head on cue, runs back to his bag and exits the room.

"It would seem as if he has more pressing things to do at the moment."

"I gathered as much," Naima said giggling softly, while looking over at Kaden as he brought the mail to her. "Mommy time just isn't what it used to be."

"He'll be back, if he's anything like his dad, he won't be able to stand not being around you for long periods of time." Skeptically shaking her head, Naima listened as Kaden continued, "You know us men, we always come back."

"Ain't that the truth?" Naima laughed, while looking over the mail.

Looking down at her, Kaden could feel nothing but love for this woman. His whole world was wrapped up in her. "How are you feeling today?"

Laying the mail on top of the novel in her lap, Naima took a hesitant pause thinking of the best way to answer his question. Her recovery had definitely been a rough one over the last five years, it was touch and go there for a while. Every time she thought about that fateful night, she got angry. Emeri almost made her lose the opportunity to see her children grow up. She took away her ability to have any more and even though her wounds had healed, that is a pain that will forever be etched in her heart. Naima thanked God everyday that she had Namiyah and Kalani so early in her life, at least she already had them as a part of her world before the hell storm known as Emeri surfaced.

"Tough question?" Kaden asked, leaning his shoulder on the wall.

"No, it wasn't tough," Naima said smiling over at him, "stop being impatient. Give me a second please. I was thinking of a response to it." She couldn't help laughing. "Haven't you learned by now, that women cannot be rushed?"

Pushing off the wall to join her on the chaise, Kaden moved the book she was reading and the mail to the floor. Wrapping his arms around her, entangling her into a hug Naima leaned into him to enjoy the closeness.

"I wasn't trying to rush you Mocha," Kaden said as he placed a kiss on her forehead, "Just trying to check on you."

Closing her eyes and enjoying the pure smell, feel and sound of him; Naima was getting drunk off his presence. Everything about Kaden was still intoxicating to her and they were sixteen years into their relationship. Fourteen of which they had been husband and wife, and while it hadn't always been wonderful, it had definitely been interesting.

"I know, and I love that you are always checking on me." Taking a deep breath Naima continued, "Today has been a good day." Making a slight grunting noise, motioning toward the other side of the chaise, "I'm about sick of using that walker to get around though. My physical therapist said that I'm getting stronger and pretty soon I may not need it anymore. I'm looking forward to that day."

"That's excellent news. I know how that has been stressing you. See," he said rising off the chaise, "that's a cause for celebration."

Laughing, "Babe, what are we celebrating? I still have to use the thing for the time being."

Bending down, to scoop her up off the chaise, into his arms, "We're celebrating the fact that you never give up. I'm sure in the hospital it would have been so easy to let go of this life, but you fought through it and I'm always going to be grateful you did."

Feeling the mist developing behind her eyes, she met Kaden's gaze head on, "Giving up was never an option. I had to fight through it, for my family. Emeri will not destroy us."

The sad reality was she almost did. Naima's mother and father were still struggling to come to grips with the situation. Naima had to hand it to her mother, she is a strong woman. Her life has been flipped, turned, twisted, pulled, yanked and she still hangs in there, giving it her all. Naima couldn't imagine how it must have felt for her to almost lose her and have the responsible party be her sister. That is one feeling that she never wanted to experience in her life. Same for her father, he's been torn in half. Naima knew how much he loved her, but he was Emeri's father too. Who knows what kind of internal turmoil consumed him.

As for Naima, she had been praying about the Emeri situation. It would be so easy to give into hating her, so easy. But, hating her would kill Naima's spirit and she couldn't have that happen. For her children's sake, she could not allow this situation to make her bitter. Her children deserve a happy mother and to grow up in a household full of laughter and love. Vengeance would not reside in her heart. She would not allow it. It's a little easier to try and forgive Emeri knowing that she wasn't the likely target.

She had pretty much put herself in the way.

Giving into her father's demands, she had agreed to meet with Emeri because part of her felt sorry for Emeri. Emeri had suffered through so much pain and was slowly allowing malice to kill her. Maybe if Emeri could see that Naima was able to forgive her. Before she had become a mother, Naima probably would never have been able to forgive her, but becoming one had softened her and Emeri needed someone to love her. Naima recognized a cry for help when she saw one, and Emeri was practically screaming for it. The real question was could Naima put her heart and soul into it? Emeri did need someone. Naima felt like maybe she wasn't dealt the best hand and needed an ally somewhere. She was just trying to figure out within herself, if she was that person. Naima could honestly say that God had been working on her and through her to help her deal with the crazy events that continue to take place in her chaotic life, but was it enough?

The Meeting

This moment is the one that Naima had been dreading and trying to avoid. Seated in the basement, sitting across from Emeri, part of her wanted to strangle the girl, the other part wanted to hug her. Sometimes she wished she didn't have such a compassionate side. She definitely got it from her Momma. Even now, after everything that has happened to their family and her, her mom was still defending Emeri. Her mother truly did love and forgive with a Jesus heart, because at what point is Emeri responsible for her actions?

Coleen, Emeri's therapist, was there as well, trying to keep the peace, Naima imagined and play mediator. Her "sister" and she used that term loosely, was sitting there without a care in the world, as if something were wrong with the rest of them and she wasn't the crazy one.

This was pretty much Coleen's show. She was trying her best to engage the entire family. However, that can be pretty difficult when the responsible party is too busy acting indifferent.

"Emeri," Coleen began again, "would you like to start off our first family session today with any words?"

"No, actually I wouldn't."

Visibly unnerved, Coleen redirected the question to the rest of the family. "Do any of you have anything to say to Emeri?"

"Actually, I do." Naima said, raising her finger up to take the floor. "I would like for Emeri to explain herself. I feel like she owes this family some sort of explanation. I mean, we didn't know who she was or where she came from and we accepted her, no questions asked." Turning to look directly into Emeri's eyes, Naima's own eyes began to water, "I always wanted a sister. It seems like such a twist of fate that God brought you into my life and the sister I always wanted put me in the hospital fighting for my life."

"Naima, you jumped in front of a bullet. It was never my intent for you to get hurt."

Narrowing her eyes at Emeri, Naima was pissed off, "Are you going to sit there, and actually attempt to defend your actions?" she eyed Emeri incredulously. She couldn't believe the nerve of this girl. She was unbelievable.

Gazing at her with pure hatred in her eyes, Emeri didn't respond.

"Naima, I think that is a valid question." Turning to Emeri,

Coleen continued, "Emeri, what do you think about the question Naima just asked you?"

The pause in the air lasted so long that Naima began to wonder if Emeri intended to respond or if she was planning to ignore Coleen. Finally, she broke her silence.

"You have no idea what my life was like, how could you?" She glanced up at Naima then and that was when Naima noticed the tears glistening in her luminous eyes. Who knew Emeri had enough emotion inside of her to shed tears.

"You have no idea what it's like not to grow up like a princess and not have two parents dote on you. You don't know what it's like to watch your mom struggle to make ends meet because her family has disowned her and she's trying to raise a child alone." She genuinely looked defeated. If Naima didn't know how evil Emeri could be, she would have fallen for her little act.

"Your brain probably cannot begin to comprehend what it is like to go to school fulltime, graduate at the top of my class and work seven days a week to help take the burden off my Mama. No idea what it is like to have no one to turn to, even your Mama, when something is consuming your life. None of you can relate to me. So, in response to your question, I'm not defending my actions, I just don't feel the need to justify you with an answer."

That's it. Just like that, Emeri had shut them all down. The frustration on Coleen's face was evident. Everyone thought the first session had been a bust until their Dad spoke. In true Kenneth fashion, he spoke softly, but firmly. "Emeri, I'm sorry." No other words did he utter from his lips. The tears that Emeri had hid beneath her eyelids came flowing down her face. And for an infinite space in time, Emeri was human. You could see the hurt and raw emotion on her face. Something about their

Dad made Emeri's defenses crumble and you could almost, like her….almost. Then reality would set in and you remember what this girl is capable of.

Naima's mother jumped up and went to her, trying to console her. This is what irritated Naima the most about her mom. She was too nice. Everyone babied Emeri. That's part of what was wrong with her now. It's as if everyone forget that Naima was sitting in a wheelchair and needed to use a walker whenever she wanted to take a few steps. They're forgetting that for the last five years, she'd been unable to run around with her children. Those are moments that she would never get back. Naima's children will never have those memories and Emeri is the one that denied them of that.

Fixating her eyes on the spectacle taking place before her, Naima watched Emeri soaking up the attention for the few tears she shed. Emeri thought that she was so smart, but she didn't have Naima fooled. Naima could see right through her, she always could. Maybe because they did share some of the same blood, Naima knew certifiable crazy when she saw it and Emeri was definitely that person. However, Emeri had made one mistake, she had underestimated her adversary. She had taken away Naima's ability to have more children. Once upon a time, Naima had wanted a house full of kids, that dream was shattered now and she vowed that Emeri would not get away with what she did to Naima and the family. Naima had never believed in an eye for an eye, until now.

Lying in bed after the kids lay down for the night, Kaden had just set foot in the house and already he was heading into the shower. As good, as things had been lately Naima was doing her best to ignore the signs. But once a man cheats on you, a third sense is developed about these things. You always know when something ain't right and something just ain't right. Her intuition was kicking into fifth gear, and though she couldn't put my finger on it, she knew that it was only a matter of time before once again, everything would hit the fan.

Chapter 4

Interlude

I hate that Mama works all the time. It left me under the care of our neighbor Mr. CT. I'm not sure of his whole name, that's just what he told me and Mama when he first moved next door. He was pleasant enough to look at and at first, he used to come over and play with me while Mama cooked him dinner since he was the only single man on the block. I used to love our time together, but then Mama picked up another job and asked Mr. CT to start watching me and in the beginning that was cool too. But, slowly things started to change. He started to touch me in places and told me if I ever told Mama he would kill her. I didn't like him after that first time.

Now he was back for more. Him with his insatiable appetite and once again, I knew what was in store for me. He could have me physically, but he would never have me mentally or emotionally.

Damir had it coming. Emeri had no idea what he was trying to prove acting like an asshole by having the letters she had written for him while cooped in the asylum rejected by the forwarding mail system. But trust, she was more than equipped to play his game. It had taken some digging to find out where he had moved too. The old house must have offered up too many unpleasant memories for him to deal with. Not that she gave a shit. He is about to learn, "There is no getting away from me," Emeri thought, "I am like God, you may not be able to see me, but I am everywhere."

Pushing her sunglasses further up her face as she turned the radio down, she watched him pick his daughter up from school. It was only a matter of time before he was in my life again, he still wanted her, she could feel it. If he would have just let her explain, she would be able to guarantee it. Sliding down in her seat, so he wouldn't see her as he drove by, she tried to think of the best way to approach him, especially since the court had ordered her to stay far away from him and his family. She needed to think of a course of action and she needed to do it fast.

"Damir."

He turned trying to see who was calling him in the darkness. His eyes lit up when he saw that it was her .

"Hey, what are you doing out here hiding in the bushes? Why don't you come inside?"

"I was trying to get myself together."

"Well," He inquired, "are you done?"

Running up to meet him on the front step Emeri replied, "I sure am."

"Good, because I have plans for you tonight and they don't involve lurking outside in the darkness. They involve lurking inside in the darkness." He said with a smile as he pushed the door open and led her into his house.

Moaning softly, "Lurking inside the darkness with you sounds like heaven."

"Excuse me Miss., but you can't park here." Startled out of her daydream by a crossing guard pounding on her windshield, Emeri put the car in gear and drove down the street.

Sitting in the family room when Naima entered assisted by her walker, Emeri could almost feel sorry for her, she was a pitiful sight to see, trying so hard to regain the full use of her legs and all. But, since she could care less about Naima anyway, fuck her.

Emeri knew that her moving back in with the family was killing Naima. She could see it in her eyes every time she came over to drop off or pick up Namiyah and Kalani. She keeps this up and it's going to be like we say in New York, hands and feet time. Clucking her teeth, Emeri just stared at Naima; she had been waiting to give her what she had been inadvertently asking for, but even Emeri didn't feel it was fair to pick on an unworthy opponent. She would wait until Naima was completely well again.

Ma Cyn walked into the family room followed by Naima's children. Kalani ran over by the fireplace to retrieve his book bag and ran right back out of the room. Namiyah however, was another story. Emeri's gaze slowly ran up and down Namiyah, she knew that Namiyah didn't like her. At fifteen, Emeri knew she had to watch this little heifa. Namiyah was never rude if she had to speak to her, Ma Cyn made sure of that, but when she and Emeri's gaze met, Emeri could feel the hatred radiating through her. Watching Namiyah from the corner of her eye, she didn't trust her for a minute; the streets of New York had trained her to recognize a threat and Namiyah was definitely a threat. She was on get back for what had happened to her mom, Emeri prayed the little girl wasn't a fool and hoped to God she didn't have to take her out, but if the heifa jumped, that is exactly what was going to happen.

Eyeing Emeri as she entered the room behind Gram Ma Cyn, Namiyah looked at her with disdain in her eyes. She hated the sight of her, and to think, this was her Aunt, the same Aunt that had almost killed her mother. Every time they came into close proximity of one another Namiyah wanted to do her bodily harm. She could tell that Emeri knew it too; Namiyah could see the crazy Emeri tried to down play, but she didn't fool Namiyah or her mom. "Mommy knows this chick is crazy too." She thought.

"Hello Emeri."

"Hi, Ma Cyn," Emeri was happy that Ma Cyn hadn't begun to treat her any differently after everything that had gone down. Ma Cyn turned to look at Namiyah, "Namiyah, did you speak?"

Namiyah almost swallowed her tongue, she had not intended on speaking to Emeri, but since Gram Ma Cyn had put her on blast, she knew that she didn't have a choice. It was either speak or get a serious talking to from Gram Ma Cyn and she definitely didn't want that.

"Hey." She managed to huff out, she heard Emeri reply but she was already back to tuning her out. She had nothing whatsoever to say to that person.

"Namiyah? Can we talk?" Pretending not to here Emeri addressing her, Namiyah went over to grab her purse off the sofa.

"Namiyah."

Turning at the brash tone, "Yes, Gram."

"Chile, I know you heard Emeri talking to you, don't be rude."

Properly chided, Namiyah dropped her head, "Yes, ma'am."

Turning as she began to exit the room, "I'll leave you two to talk." Glancing over her shoulder before she was completely out of the room; looking directly at Namiyah, "Are you ok?"

"Yes, I'm fine."

"Ok, honey, I'll be right in the kitchen if you need me." She said as she hummed her way down the hall.

Namiyah had to smile at that. Gram was always in the kitchen, cooking up some delicious concoction. Twisting her face into a frown, she would rather be anywhere but right here having to deal with Emeri's nonsense. She wasn't as nice as her Mom and Gram. She didn't have extra breath to waste on garbage.

Turning to face Emeri and give her undivided attention, she spoke quickly and harshly,

"What do you want?"

"Now, now, is that any way to talk to your favorite Auntie."

Namiyah almost laughed out loud at that, "You're reaching, even for yourself. I don't even like you, so suggesting you are a favorite anything is beyond hilarious," Cocking her head to the side, Namiyah was getting more upset by the minute, especially since she had to repeat herself.

"What do you want? In case in your deluded mind you were too dumb to understand the question you were asked the first time."

Emeri jumped up off the chaise, "Excuse me, but who do you think you're talking to? I am still your Aunt and an adult; you will not speak to me like that."

Namiyah snorted as she broke into laughter, "Aunt, by default and adult, not hardly. Your age makes you an adult, not your mentality. You may think I'm only a teenager, but I can read you like a book and you are a joke. You don't fool me. I can see right through you."

Emeri could feel the tension racing through her body, Namiyah had to learn a lesson and she was going to have to be the one to teach her and put this little girl in her place. Racing across the room and snatching Namiyah's long, curly ponytail, Emeri pulled it so hard Namiyah's eyes began to water and she honestly thought Emeri was going to pull her hair out roots and all.

Seeing the tears in her eyes, Emeri exposed a slow smile. Leaning down to whisper in Namiyah's ear, "I see now that we understand who is in charge and who isn't. I don't want to have to hurt you Namiyah, but I will. Stay out of my way; this is the only warning that you will receive." Abruptly letting Namiyah's ponytail go, Namiyah fell to the floor as Emeri left the room.

Grabbing her head Namiyah couldn't understand how someone of Emeri's size could have so much strength. Looking around on the floor, she fully expected to see her hair lying around her, but miraculously it was all still intact. Slowly rising to her feet Namiyah could feel the dull beginnings of a headache. Emeri thought she was so smart, but so did Lucifer, until he was cast out of Heaven. Emeri was going to have her day of judgment; she was going to see to it.

Sitting in her room at her desk that night, Namiyah was researching ways to effectively kill someone without a trace of evidence. There had to be some way to eliminate Emeri without going to jail for it. She didn't think the judge would buy the fact that she just plain hated her as a valid excuse. Receiving a knock on her bedroom door, Namiyah minimized the computer screen.

"Yes, come in." It was her Mom.

"Hey Muffin, I came to check on you before I went to bed."

Even after all this time, Namiyah had to hide the urge to cry whenever she saw her Mom assisted by her walker. It just wasn't fair; her Mom had always been the sweetest, most wonderful person. Sometimes she got so angry with God for allowing this to happen to her family. One family should not have to go through everything that they had been through.

"Hi Mommy." She stood up to help her Mom into the room so she could leave her walker in the hallway. The good thing was her Mom really was getting better at walking and you could tell she wouldn't need her walker for much longer. Guiding her to the bed so she could sit, Namiyah made sure she was comfortable before she sat back in the chair at her desk.

"I wanted to talk to you for a little bit. Gram told me that you and Emeri chatted today," raising an inquiring eyebrow at Namiyah, "I know how your temper can be, how did that go?"

Glancing down, pulling an imaginary piece of lint off her pajamas, Namiyah thought of the best way to answer that question and decided instead to ask one of her own.

"Mom, can you answer something for me that I don't understand?"

"Sure, baby. Shoot away."

"Why is everyone so accepting of Emeri? After everything that she has done, how can everyone act like life is normal and all is ok?" Feeling the tears she had fought so hard not to show come down her face, Namiyah continued, "You're moving around on a walker, which is a constant reminder of what she did to you and even you talk to her. I hate her for what she did to you and for what she did to us. When you suffered, Kalani and I suffered too. It's not fair, she should not be allowed to come back and have her life be ok."

"Come sit next to me honey." Naima opened her arms as Namiyah came over joining her on the bed and burying her face into Naima's chest as she cried her heart out. Gently running her fingers through Namiyah's wavy hair, "You know it is not our job to judge anyone. You have to remember that Emeri has no family but us. We can't leave her on her own, when it's so obvious that she needs a strong family structure to help her get her act together."

Raising her head to stare into her Mom's hazel eyes, "But Mommy, she could have killed you, why don't you hate her?"

Naima thought long and hard before she answered. Namiyah had valid points, but it didn't change what was, no matter how she felt about the situation, Naima had to teach her child right from wrong.

"Almost, doesn't mean succeeded and she didn't even get close to my spirit." Reaching down placing her hand underneath Namiyah's chin, "My spirit and relationship with God help me get through and that's the most honest answer I can give you. I used to be very angry with Emeri, but I don't hate her. I pray that God continually helps me to forgive her and make peace with the whole situation." Wiping her baby girl's tears, "and I hope that you ask Him to do the same for you. Ok?" she asked kissing the top of her head, "Make your peace with this Muffin, otherwise it will consume you."

Closing her eyes slowly as she let her Mom's words digest, Namiyah couldn't understand her point. She wanted to, but her mother was too nice sometimes, this was a situation that warranted action and Emeri would get hers.

Opening her eyes, she tightened her arms around her Mom. "Thank you for the talk, I do feel a little better."

"Glad to hear it." Taking a small breath, "Well Muffin, I have to kiss Kalani good night. Will you help your Momma to her walker?"

"Gimme a kiss so I can leave you be for the night." Her Mom said as Namiyah was helping her up.

Doing as told, Namiyah placed a kiss on her Mom's cheek and watched her as she slowly made her way down the hall to Kalani's room. Retreating back into her room and closing her door, Namiyah pulled up the web page she'd been reading before her Mom stopped by her room. There had to be something on the page that would be beneficial to her and she wasn't going to rest until she discovered what it was.

Chapter 5

"Alanna, let's go." Damir was barely able to contain his smile as his baby girl came racing into the foyer to meet him at the door.

"Daddy, where are we going this time?" she asked as she held her arms out, so he could help put her jacket on.

"Remember, I told you that we were going to visit a friend of mine today?"

Looking up at him with big brown baby doll eyes, she replied. "Uh huh."

"Do you want to bring a toy with you? You can only bring one."

She shook her head, "No, I don't need a toy."

"Ok, baby girl. Let's hit it." Damir said as he guided them out the door.

Consumed in his own thoughts as he drove, Damir could not believe that it had been five years since his life had taken such a drastic turn, in some ways better, in some ways worse. Alanna was the silver lining to his world. She was too young to even begin to comprehend that she had saved him from himself. At one point, depression was threatening to take him out of this world and he still fought with it at times. She was his reason to not give into it though; it is because of her that he was.

Observing Alanna through the rearview mirror, Damir couldn't get over how much she resembled Amber. Sometimes he sat and wondered if Amber's attitude toward children would have changed once she had gotten an opportunity to hold them in her arms. Because, he was in love with Alanna from the moment, he'd lain eyes on her and then when the nurse placed her in his waiting arms, the deal was forever sealed. Damir knew on the spot that he would die for her. Anything that she needed he would provide, she would never want for anything.

Pulling into the driveway and parking at their destination, the anticipation was enough to choke him.

"Come on baby girl, we're here."

"Is this where your friend lives?" Alanna asked as she unbuckled her seat belt.

Coming around to open her car door for her, Damir responded, "It sure is."

"Cool." She said.

Pressing the buzzer for the doorbell once they reached the door, he became a little apprehensive, a trait that he was not accustomed too.

The door opened then, "Hi stranger."

Damir was in shock at the image that greeted him. Nothing could have prepared him for this.

"Cat got your tongue?" She laughed. There it was. Her laugh put him at ease. It was the same honey coated laugh that he had fallen in love with years before.

Pulling her into a gentle hug as to not crush her, he was caught off guard by how fragile she seemed.

"Naima, it has been too long."

"It definitely has been." Pulling out of his embrace, "Who is this little one?" she asked.

Grabbing her hand, "This little one is my baby girl, Alanna."

Bending down awkwardly so that they were eye level, Naima held out her hand and Alanna grasped it, "Hi Alanna, I'm Ms. Naima, it's nice to meet you."

"Hi, Ms. Naima." She said shyly as she wrapped her free arm around Damir's leg.

Holding onto her walker as she struggled to stand up again, Damir moved to help her, she waved him off.

"I have it. I'm just a little slow. The normal everyday activities don't hurt as much as they used to."

"Still, maybe you should sit down for a little bit."

"I won't argue with you there. Ya'll come on in. Is it ok if Alanna plays with Kalani? He's doing his homework, but I'm sure that he will welcome the interruption."

Damir looked down at his princess, who was still clutching his leg for dear life, and started to say no, she would stay with him, but Kalani came bouncing in the room at that moment and her little eyes lit up, and then the two of them were off.

"Oh-oh," Damir said, looking up at Naima, "Do I detect the beginnings of a crush? My feelings are a little hurt. She didn't say bye Daddy or anything."

Laughing lightly, "Awww, is this the first time she chose a guy over you? Don't worry it gets harder the older they get. Kalani favors his teacher and every time it kills me a little inside when he runs away from me to get to her." Naima shined sympathetic eyes at Damir, "Do you need a hug to get through this difficult time?"

Chuckling softly, "No, I think I'll survive."

Making herself comfortable on the sofa, Naima pointed to the love seat opposite her.

"Have a seat."

Doing as commanded, Damir felt awkward. He had no idea what to talk to her about. Gratefully, he need not have worried; she was more than amped and ready.

"Damir, I apologize for not seeing you prior to today." Taking a deep breath, "It's just that in all honesty, I had no idea what to say. I didn't know if you blamed me for what took place that fateful night on your birthday. I was more so at a loss. I wanted to reach out to you but I couldn't for my own selfish reasons, and for that I do apologize."

Thinking about all that he had been through in the last five years, Damir blamed myself more than he blamed anyone else. It was his selfish actions that helped push Emeri off the deep end. One moment of mindless pleasure had cost him his future wife and one of his children. He would never forgive himself for that. The guilt was his to bear and his alone.

Quietly responding to her, "I never blamed you. You brought peace to my life. I was the one that screwed up and I screwed up big."

"Well, you won't get an argument from me there. Emeri is a beautiful woman; I can certainly understand how a man could slip up. If only she used her powers for good."

"How have you and your family been holding up from the strain of it all?"

"As well as can be expected, I guess. Emeri is back at my parent's house because she has nowhere else to go. My parents are trying to figure it out; their marriage is under enormous strain. I think that this is the most difficult situation they have had to endure together and it is definitely taking its toll."

"And you," Damir asked her, "How are you doing?"

Pausing for a minute and then sighing audibly, "I'm angry. I'm so angry, I can't even begin to articulate all the raging emotions that I have been dealing with since one bullet changed my whole life." Suddenly raising her hands to her mouth she looked mortified, "I am so sorry, how thoughtless of me. Your life was drastically altered by one bullet as well. The real question is, how are you doing? My life is pretty much intact, you are the one that lost so much that evening.

Damir shrugged, "Hey, I'm living. Alanna makes life bearable. It's hard to be depressed when you have this awesome, spitting image of Amber smiling up at you. I can't help but be grateful for all that I have."

Rising off the love seat to sit next to Naima on the sofa, he took one of her hands into his, "I know that one of my biggest regrets is letting you go." He brought her hand to his lips to receive the kiss he wanted to place on her lips. Damir could not rationalize how he had willingly walked away from this woman.

"Damir, that's sweet." She said removing her hand from his grasp. "But what was then and what is now, are two different things."

Gently placing his hand under her chin and guiding her face toward his, he could tell by her hazel eyes that she was afraid of what she was feeling and wanted to run away from him. But Damir was not going to allow that. Kissing her softly at first and then more so with a sense of urgency, he wanted all of her, right here and now and he wasn't alone. She was now responding to him and for that space in time; it was as it was when they first met years ago.

The front door closing abruptly jarred them out of the magic they were creating. Jumping up as Kaden walked into the room, Damir turned to face the wall to gather his composure. Kaden walked over to Naima and kissed the lips that Damir had just reacquainted myself with, and then Kaden spoke to him.

Reaching his hand out to shake his, "Hey man, I didn't know that you were dropping by today."

"Yeah," Damir said taking his hand, "I stopped by for a long overdue visit to see Naima, to see how she was holding up for myself."

Tightening his grip on Damir's hand, Kaden narrowed his eyes. Damir tightened his grip as well. Staring him down, silently asking if he really wanted to start this right here, right now. At the end of the day, he was still his boss. Kaden would do well to remember that. Seeing that Damir wasn't going to back down, Kaden released his hand and left the room. Calling up to Alanna, Damir knew that he had over stayed his welcome. It was time for them to go.

Damir could clearly envision the bodily damage he was going to inflict on Emeri. It's was clear to him that even a court system can't control Emeri's crazy ass. The girl kept popping up everywhere. Coincidence, doubt it. When the shootout first went down at his birthday extravaganza, Damir had wanted to murder Emeri. It had taken a lot of prayer and his parents stepping in to help him get through. Seeing as they had also lost a child to a senseless occurrence, they knew exactly what he was going through. His Mother was thrilled when she discovered that Damir had named his baby girl Alanna. She had been such a blessing to him, especially since Alanna no longer had a mother figure around; his Mom had been a Godsend and Alanna adored her, the two of them have their own special bond. Alanna offered his Mother an opportunity to have a chance to right the wrongs she had made with Damir's little sister.

Chapter 6

Interlude

*T*oday Mama is working late again. I tried to stay as late as I could at school but all of my study sessions are over now, there was nowhere to go but home and all I want to do is cry. Mr. CT would be waiting for me...again. It was already going on seven o'clock and school let out at three. I'm sure he has to be wondering where I am.

Slowly walking up the porch steps to the front door, Mr. CT was waiting when I walked in.

"It's late. Where have you been?" he asked as he beckoned her to the kitchen to eat dinner.

Removing my backpack and placing it on the floor, I eased my way over to the dinner table.

"I had a study group after school today. When it ended, I came straight home."

"Ok, well eat up. We have a long night ahead of us." I cringed at his statement. I knew exactly what kind of long night he had in mind. My Mama and I prayed to God every night and she was a firm believer in him. But if he was real, why was he allowing this to happen to me? Maybe he hadn't heard my other prayers.

"God, if you are listening and if you are real, please stop Mr. CT from what he is doing to me. Please. Amen."

After dinner, I was trying my best to stay busy. I had washed all the dishes and the kitchen was clean. Now I was in my room sketching a photo of me and my friends. I love to draw; it puts me in a zone and takes me away from the real world, sort of like a retreat. No sooner had I gotten my outline of us down on paper good, there was a knock at my door. I didn't want to let him in, but knew I didn't really have a choice.

"Come in." I said as unenthusiastic as possible hoping he would get the hint to leave me alone.

Entering with two wine glasses and a bottle of white wine, he grinned at me. I was disgusted.

"Care to have a drink with me?"

"Mr. CT, why do we go through this every time, you know I'm not old enough to drink."

"Oh, come on now. I won't tell your Mom if you won't."

"I don—"

"Emeri, you'll have a drink. Do you understand?" He said interrupting me. Gone was his pleasant demeanor he was all business now.

Pushing my artwork to the side, I grabbed the wine glass he was offering me. There was no sense in fighting the inevitable. Anything I did Mr. CT used against me and to his advantage. Last time I fought him, he left bloody teeth marks down the left side of my stomach.

Smiling as I took the glass, he said, "Good, I'm glad we

understand each other." Walking over to my stereo, he turned on some slow jams. Coming back over to join me on the bed he raised his glass of wine and took a sip.

"How about a strip tease for me tonight?"

I must have looked at him like he had lost his mind because he back handed me so hard I swore my eye balls were two seconds from popping out of my sockets. Though I didn't drop my wine glass, there were now drops of wine running down my hand and the front of my jeans.

"Drink up so you can dance for Daddy."

Daddy my ass, I hope that he is no one's "Daddy". A real Daddy would not act like this, I'm sure of it. I may not have one, but I've seen my friends with their fathers and it is nothing like this. Lifting my glass of wine and sucking down the whole thing, I asked for another, to which he promptly filled it to the brim. Maybe if I drink as much as possible I will have no recollection of tonight and it will be over before I know it. After downing the second glass and holding out my glass for more, he refused me.

"I think you've had enough of that. I want you to be able to focus on dancing for me." Pushing me to my feet and laying back on my bed, I had his undivided attention. This was the first time he had asked me to dance. I had no idea what to do.

"Come on, what's the problem. Don't you know how to dance? Move your hips to the beat of the music." Tears started rolling down my face as my hips slowly found the beat.

"Unbutton your shirt as you move." Closing my eyes so I wouldn't have to look at him, I did as I was told. Reaching the last button, I left it open and continued to sway to the music.

Getting off the bed to stand behind me, Mr. CT grabbed my shirt pulling it down my arms until it hit the floor. Moving my *hair to the side he kissed the back of my neck. Eyes still closed a fresh wave of tears made their way down my cheeks. I was a prisoner inside my own body. Turning me in his arms to face him, he undid the button of my jeans and pushed my zipper down. Backing me onto the bed he pulled the jeans down my legs, past my colorful undies that said Tuesday, though it was Wednesday.*

Why couldn't my Mama come home early just once? Just one time so she could save me. Mr. CT's breathing began to change, I could tell that he was getting excited. Consumed in my own thoughts, I didn't even realize that he already had me out my cute little undies. Lowering his head to lick the inside of my thigh, I tried one more time to plead with God. "Please, please God, make him stop. I'll stop picking on Nicole in school. It's not her fault that she looks like a praying mantis. I'll do anything; just make Mr. CT leave me alone. Amen.

God must have been on vacation because my prayer went unanswered that night. Once again, Mr. CT got what he wanted and no one could rescue me. As far as I'm concerned God does not exist because if he did he would have saved me and he did not. I'm done with prayer and I'm done with God.

The light from the computer monitor illuminated Emeri's devious smile. She could not believe her good fortune. She had finally cracked the code and hacked into the court's case files.

"Damn," she thought, "I am a fuckin' genius. The FBI needs to recruit my ass; I could teach them a thing or two."

Visibly pleased with herself, Emeri began searching for her information in the systems database. "Ah, here we go," muttering to herself as her eyes lit up like a Christmas tree when she found what she was looking for. "Let's see what they have in here about me." Scrolling through the records, she pulled the most recent notes from her sessions with Coleen. "Hmmmn, let's see what the good Doctor has been saying."

Coleen's Notes: 11:00 AM Session

Emeri seems to be regressing. She refuses to take responsibility for the actions that resulted in her incarceration and is in a state of denial. I am of the opinion that Emeri is suffering from a deeper issue that we have yet to tap into. Growing up without a father in her life has caused her to lash out at almost everyone around her, with the exception of her stepmother Cynthia Vaughn. Cynthia seems to hold a place in Emeri's heart that no one else can reach. This could be a result of the loss of her mother and needing to identify with that motherly influence in her life.

I am also of the opinion that Emeri suffers from an advanced stage of sibling rivalry. For whatever reason only known to her, she has declared war on her half sister Naima Fairchild. There is an underlying sense of resentment between Naima and Emeri because in Emeri's mind Naima grew up with everything that Emeri images a family is supposed to have.

After evaluating Emeri Castado during this last session, it is in my doctor's opinion that

Emeri needs to be monitored till further notice.
I do not believe she is ready to rejoin society
and is a threat to herself and to others.

Emeri could not believe what she just read. No that evil witch
didn't. So Coleen was trying to get her put back into the psych
ward at jail. She would not stand for it. Coleen would have to be
dealt with and immediately.

Reaching for the phone on her desk as it began to ring; Emeri
was not pleased with the interruption. "Hello."

"Emeri!" Camille said as soon as she heard her voice on
the other end of the line saying hello, "Why haven't you called
me?"

"Camille calm down and don't be yelling at me." Emeri took
the phone away from her ear looking at it in disgust. Camille
must have lost her mind talking to her like that. Least they all
forget who I am she thought.

"I'm sorry. I didn't mean to yell. I just haven't heard from
you since you've been out of jail." Emeri could sense that she
was two seconds from pouting, "Did you forget about me?"

Not in the mood to deal with Camille's sob fest at the
moment, Emeri wanted to scream, I have more pressing things
to do. "Camille, seriously, I don't have time for this. You have
got to get a grip. I've been busy." Her patience was thin. Even
though Camille had been one of her only visitors in jail, Emeri
didn't feel as if she owed the girl all her time.

"Well fine, don't allow me to take up any more of your day."

Emeri hung up without responding, wondering if Camille
was going to be a problem. She seemed harmless enough, but
sometimes you never know about people.

Shifting her thoughts back to Coleen, she tried to think of what to do about her. Not that it wasn't easy enough to change her notes in the database it was just that once notes had been entered into the system Coleen had it set up that they automatically got sent to her parole officer as well, so any attempts to change the notes would be futile. But it was obvious that Coleen was against her, maybe it was time to pay the good Doctor a visit.

After trailing Coleen for the past couple of weeks, Emeri finally had enough ammunition to set her world on fire and she couldn't wait.

Walking through the necessary security points, it felt good to be on the other side of the system looking in. Even still, Emeri hated everything about the jail, though she was out on parole, she would rather not have to come to this place, but this is where Coleen was and so this is where she would be as well.

Coleen was exactly where Emeri knew she would be, in her office going over paperwork. Standing in the doorway undetected observing her, Coleen looked like she was about to pass out. Reaching in her desk drawer to pull out a cigarette and lighter, she leaned back in her chair taking in a massive puff from her cancer stick. That puff must have given her extreme pleasure; her face displayed one of pure ecstasy.

Stepping into the office and shutting the door behind her, Emeri watched as the ecstasy previously displayed on Coleen's face was replaced by one of shock.

"Hello Coleen."

Immediately putting her cigarette out and sitting up in her chair, she gave Emeri her full attention.

"Emeri," she started, while shifting paperwork to locate her desk calendar, "I don't have you scheduled for an appointment today, and so what do I owe the honor of this visit?"

Making her way to the empty chair in front of Coleen's desk, Emeri took her time answering as she made herself comfortable.

"Well Coleen, I've been thinking," stopping to give her the once over before continuing, "you shouldn't be my therapist anymore."

"Oh, is that all," Coleen waved her hand in the air blatantly attempting to disregard Emeri, "Unfortunately Emeri, I was court appointed. You don't have a say in the matter, though I will gladly put a note in your file."

Laughing in spite of herself, Emeri thought Coleen was too cute, because she honestly thought that she had a choice.

"No see, I think you misunderstood," raising her eyebrow, Coleen remained silent as Emeri continued, "You will tell the judge that you are no longer able to work on this case due to conflict of interest issues."

Slowly rising to her feet, Coleen was beyond pissed off, but she was well trained to deal with the Emeri's of the world and so remained calm, "I have no idea what you are talking about, but if you'll excuse me," she pointed toward the door, "I have an appointment coming in momentarily that I need to prepare for."

Emeri rose as well. Leaning across Coleen's desk till their faces were inches apart, "You know exactly what I am talking about," she hissed, "You should really give some serious thought to the actions you take moving forward." Pulling her sunglasses out of her purse as she gathered the rest of her things, Emeri headed toward the door, turning before she made an exit, "You've been warned."

As soon as the door was completely closed, Coleen fell back

into her chair. She wondered if Emeri knew what was going on or bluffing. After counseling Emeri for the past five years, she wasn't exactly the bluffing type. Having an unsettling feeling about the whole thing, Coleen wondered what she knew. Picking up a picture frame off her desk, the one of her and her son at his recent birthday party, she lovingly ran her finger over his chubby cheeks, I can't put my son in danger. Picking up the phone, she called the judge's assistant and asked to be reassigned as Emeri's therapist. Hanging up the phone after confirming the switch, she still couldn't rest easy; something Emeri said didn't sit right with her. What exactly did Emeri know?

Chapter 7

"Just a few more steps, come on, you can do it. You're almost there."

Sweat was profusely sliding down Naima's body, but she willed her legs to listen to what her brain and physical therapist were telling them to do. Though walking was definitely getting easier, she would be lying if she said it still wasn't painful. Goodness, sometimes she wondered which was worse, childbirth, or this. Thinking about childbirth made her sad. She would never again know the joy of being pregnant and feeling her baby move and kick inside her belly for the first time. Emeri had stolen that from her.

"Naima," her therapist yelled, snapping her back to reality, "You're not concentrating."

What was she talking about? She was concentrating. Maybe not as hard as she was when they originally started, but she still was.

"Good job." Her therapist said when she reached the ending point. Naima was exhausted. For the life of her, she couldn't ever remember it being this hard to walk. Amazing how something that used to be a mindless action now caused her anxiety just thinking about it.

"You're doing a lot better. How would you feel about trading your walker in for a cane?"

Naima thought her ears must be deceiving her, as her eyes began to water. Was she really telling her that she was finally going to be able to kick her hated walker to the curb? Oh, God is so good. Next thing you know she would be walking without any assistance. Yes! She was all about it.

"Oh," Naima said breathlessly, "that would be wonderful. Please tell me that this is not a joke and you are serious."

"I am very serious. You are making excellent progress, won't be too long from now that you will no longer need the cane either. You're well on your way Missy."

She was standing close enough to her that Naima could reach out to her and place a kiss on her cheek.

"Oh, thank you, thank you, and thank you so much. I cannot wait till I can move around again unaided. Just the idea of being able to run around the yard with Kalani is enough to make me smile. I cannot wait!"

Sitting at the dinner table later that evening with Namiyah and Kalani, her mind couldn't help but wonder where Kaden was. Old habits die-hard and his were beginning to speak very loudly and become questionable again. This is how it always began every other time it turned out that he was creeping in the past and her gut was telling her that this time would be no different. She wanted to believe otherwise, but reality is reality. Kaden would never change. Her mind knew it; her heart was always trying to make up for it. Maybe that's why she didn't feel as bad about kissing Damir back that day. Though by no means was he any better than Kaden, after getting caught up in Emeri's crazy triangle, but something about his calm spirit spoke to her and seeing him with his little girl had been enough to make her heart melt.

After seeing to it that the kids were settled in their beds for the night, Naima went down to her study to call Damir, she shrugged and figured why not, boredom was kicking in and Kaden was nowhere to be found. She smiled when he answered on the first ring. It was almost as if he had been expecting her call.

"Damir here."

"Hi, it's Naima."

His tone softened when he realized who was on the other end of his phone line.

"This is a surprise. How are you?"

"I'm good. A little on the lonely side, but otherwise all is well."

"Lonely? Kaden isn't there to keep you company?"

"No, he's never here anymore. The last time I saw him was this morning. Since then I haven't been able to reach him through email or phone. Did he come into work today?"

Damir could tell he was treading on sensitive territory. "Yes, I can vouch for him. He was at work all day today."

Naima sighed with relief at that. Well where is he now then? "Thanks for that. Lately he just seems so distant, I don't know anything that is going on with him."

At a loss for words and not really wanting to talk about her husband and his employee, Damir searched for a new topic to discuss.

"Well, I'm fine by the way."

"Oh my gosh, please forgive my rudeness. I've been very self absorbed recently. I'm glad to hear that you are well. How is the little one?"

"Alanna is good. She's always running around and jumping all over the place, tearing up my house."

Naima had to laugh at that. She remembered when Namiyah and Kalani were that little. She missed that.

"Ah yes, these are the good days, enjoy them. She will be all grown up before you know it and you'll be wondering what happened to the little girl that used to run around jumping on your stuff."

"Yeah, I'm not looking forward to her getting older. I want her to stay my little girl forever. But on a more adult note, how about dinner with me?"

Almost dropping the phone, Naima was shocked; her hearing had to be going right along with her mind. Had she heard him right? Was Damir asking her on a date?

"You still there?"

Finally finding her voice, "Yes, I'm still here."

"Well, will you join me?"

"Uh," she was at a loss for words. Damir knew that she was married. Kaden still had no idea about her and Damir's past history. Would it really be wrong if two friends went out to dinner?"

Giving it some thought, Namiyah could watch Kalani since Kaden was never home anyway. Dinner was harmless enough.

"I'd love too, when did you have in mind?"

"Tomorrow."

"Tomorrow? That soon?"

"Yes, that soon. I want to see you."

"Ok, that should be fine. Where did you have in mind?"

"My place." Naima felt her stomach drop. There was no way she could go to Damir's place for dinner. That was a little too intimate for her.

"Damir, I can't come to your place for dinner. I think that would border on inappropriate."

"Naima, I'm not the big bad wolf trying to eat you as soon as you come through the door," he paused for emphasis, "Unless you want me too."

She could already feel her body reacting to his words.

"Please don't go there. I already feel a certain kind of way about this dinner."

"Relax; I just want to make you dinner, nothing else. I can have a car pick you up. Pick up at six thirty, dinner at seven? What do you think?"

He obviously was not going to take no for an answer. "Well ok," Naima said hesitantly, "I guess that will be ok."

"Great. Look at is as old friends getting reacquainted with one another."

"I guess we could call it that."

"Wonderful. I'll see you tomorrow about seven. I'm going to try and get a workout in before I hit the bed."

"Ok. See you tomorrow."

Hanging up the phone, Naima was unsure of what had just happened. She had called to chat with Damir and ended up having a dinner date with him tomorrow. How was she going to explain that if Kaden asked?

She must have thought him up, cause guess who came

whistling his way into her study right at that moment.

"Hey baby," Kaden said as he walked over and placed a kiss on top of her head.

"Hi. Late night at the office?"

"Yeah. I'm working on this project right now that keeps me there late."

Naima could not believe it. She had just caught Kaden in a lie. He had no idea that she had talked to Damir and knew that he worked his regular work hours and that was it. So, where had he been for the last few hours?

"Really? What kind of project? If you don't mind me asking."

"Oh, just sports stuff." He changed the subject, "How was your day today?" He was deliberately trying to avoid the conversation.

Fine, he could have it his way, she could now guarantee that she would have dinner with Damir tomorrow evening and not feel guilty about it.

"Today was good. My therapist said I can get a cane and get rid of that walker. I'm really excited about that. They measured me for my cane today, so as soon as it arrives, I am walker free!"

"That's good Mocha." He said kissing Naima on the cheek this time, "I'm beat. I'm going to take a shower and call it a night."

"Want me to join you?"

"I'm too tired tonight. Maybe tomorrow ok?"

"Ok." Naima was fuming. Tomorrow she would be at Damir's so Kaden could take another solo shower then too.

Damir was pulling out all the stops for tonight's dinner with Naima. He wanted everything to run smoothly. Already having dropped Alanna at his parent's house for the evening, he had a Caesar salad chilling in the refrigerator, parmesan crusted tilapia baking in the oven, rice and honey croissants already on the table and wine sitting on ice. He was ready for the night to begin. He had sent the car to pick Naima up at six thirty. Glancing at his watch it was quarter to seven now, so she should be arriving momentarily.

Picking up an oven mitt as the timer went off indicating that the fish was done, Damir took the fish out of the oven just as the door bell rang. Perfect timing he thought as he placed the fish on the table, leaving the oven mitt on the counter as he headed toward the door.

The vision that stood before him was mythical. Reminiscent of the first moment they met, Naima still commanded his attention.

"Hi." She said looking up at him with a whimsical smile.

Opening the door further making room for her and her walker to enter, Damir couldn't help staring at her. She was still and would probably always be as gorgeous as the day they met, walker and all.

"Hey, glad you could make it."

"Of course I could make it. I told you that I would come. I always do what I say I will.

"Likewise." He said as he closed the front door, "If you will follow me, dinner is ready and waiting."

Walking in front of her at a slower pace than normal so she would be able to keep up, Damir couldn't help but marvel at the crazy circumstances that kept tying them to one another. It was almost as if this was God's way of pushing them together so they would remain in each other's lives.

Holding Naima's walker in place as she slowly lowered herself into the dining chair, Damir made sure that she was comfortable before he sat down.

"Wow, you really out did yourself, everything looks so tasty."

"Thank you. Anything to please you."

"You don't need to please me. We're just two old friends catching up over dinner."

For now, he thought as he filled both of their wine glasses. He would make her see things his way before long.

Relaxing in his state of the art basement after dinner, Damir knew Naima was feeling nice. They had gone through a bottle of wine at dinner and were now working on their second bottle.

Naima was seated on his sofa; he had taken to the loveseat to give her some space as they continued to enjoy one another's company.

"Last night you made it seem like you had something on your mind while we were on the phone. Care to talk about it?"

Placing her wine glass on a coaster on his glass table, she seemed hesitant to begin.

"I don't know, things just haven't been the same at home, that's all."

"Do you want to elaborate?"

"Not really."

"Aight cool. Want to watch a movie or something?" Her face lit up at that suggestion.

"Sure, what you got?"

"Depends, what are you in the mood for?"

"A comedy, I am in the mood to laugh. Throw in a Katt Williams stand up. I think he is hilarious."

"You're in luck. I have his whole collection."

"Awesome!"

Looking at his watch, it was a little after three in the morning. Damir couldn't believe so much time had passed by. They had watched his entire Katt Williams collection, and now Naima was lying on him fast asleep. He debated long and hard about whether to carry her into one of his guest bedrooms, before finally deciding on putting her in his own bed. He couldn't help himself; he wanted her to be close to him at all times.

Taking off her clothes, changing her into one of his button down pajama tops, he pushed the covers back and placed her in bed, pulling the covers back up to her chin. Gazing down at her, she looked like a little doll while she slept he thought as he brushed her hair off of her face with his fingers. Satisfied that she was content, he grabbed his towel and headed for the shower.

Stepping into the steaming hot water, Damir was in heaven, there was nothing more relaxing and refreshing than the drops of water running over the entire length of your body. He could feel the tensions of the day melting away and in the other room was the woman that would some day be his queen; she was just unaware of that at the moment.

Turning the water off, grabbing his towel, wrapping it around his waist, he returned to his room to search for the matching pajama bottoms to the top he had put on Naima.

"Hey, what time is it." Damir jumped at the sound of Naima's sleep laced voice.

Turning to peer at her in the darkness, "It's going on four in the morning."

"Oh my goodness. I have lost my mind, I have children. They are probably worried out of their mind.

Damir found it amusing that she automatically was worried about her children, but didn't seem concerned about her husband.

"You can always call and check on them."

She looked at him like he was crazy, "At this hour, no. I'll be there when they get up in the morning for school. I do need to be getting home though. Will you have a car take me?"

"Of course I will, if that is what you want. Or," he said coming over to stand directly in front of her, "you could stay a little longer and enjoy my company." Slowly letting the towel around his waist fall to the floor, he wanted to make sure she had something to think about.

"Wow."

Damir smiled at her response. "Do I take that as confirmation that you will be staying?"

"I uh," Naima's face grew red. She could not believe that the sight of him nude was causing her to stutter. "I'm not sure that is such a good idea. I'm a married woman."

"Yeah you are, but by your own admission, you say your husband is never there any more, so what do you have to lose?"

"Um, it's just not right."

"Really? Do you always do what's right?" he asked as he gently mounted her on the bed.

Looking up at him as he straddled her, Naima knew that she was a goner. When he began kissing her collarbone that all but solidified it.

Returning home just in time to see her munchkins off to school, Naima just knew the guilt was transparent across her face. Luckily for her, Kaden was once again invisible. She could not believe it, she had been gone all night and apparently so had he. Good thing she did allow the good loving that Damir had given her not too long ago. Just the thought of it made her blush and washed away any misplaced guilt.

Chapter 8

Haven knew that she had no business driving in her advanced stage of pregnancy, but she was fed up with Chris not bringing his ass home at night. There is something to be said about hiring a private investigator. She knew he had been cheating on her, now she had concrete proof to back up her claims.

Running several lights as she drove to Naima's house, she didn't give a damn. She would just pay the tickets when they came in the mail. Naima had reluctantly agreed to come with her; she was pretty sure the reason being that she thought she had lost her mind. But she didn't care.

Screeching to a stop in front of Naima's house she beeped the horn three times before she rode down the street a little ways to buck a u-turn. Haven hated driving in DC, but once Kaden and Naima officially decided to give their marriage another go, Naima had moved herself and the kids into the house that Kaden had bought here.

Waving as she came out the door and locked it, Naima had

a huge smile on her face. Haven had to give it to her, she was definitely a trooper she thought as she watched her slowly walk to the car with her cane. Haven didn't know anyone who could endure all that Naima had endured and still be so forgiving and happy all the time.

"Hey Nai."

"Hey girl." She said as she got into the car. "Are you absolutely sure you want to do this?" Giving Haven the "look". "You know you don't have to right? We can always go eat or shop or something instead."

"Girl please, we going." Pulling off slowly waiting for her to fasten her seat belt, Haven handed her the photos from the private investigator.

Taking the photos from her, Naima was not prepared for what she saw. "Whoa, I cannot believe this. Chris always seems like the perfect gentleman."

"Oh, he's the perfect gentleman aight, for someone else that is."

"I don't know what to say."

"You don't have to say anything. It's not your fault that he's a dog."

"I think you're jumping the gun a little. You and Chris' past history isn't all that great. Maybe he has a little get back in him. Shoot, you put that man through hell."

"He said that he forgave me. We went to church and couples' counseling and everything."

"Haven, seriously stop and think about things from his point of view. You are the one responsible for putting an innocent Chris behind bars for several years. Who can forgive something of that magnitude?

"I mean, I don't know. You forgave me....right?"

"Yes, I did, but it took us a lot of counseling to get to where we are now and I still look at you sideways from time to time." She laughed giving me a pinch on my arm. "You suspect."

Playfully slapping Naima on the arm, Haven laughed, "Well damn, give me a little credit. I promised we would never go down that road again."

Naima cut her eyes at her, "I hear what your mouth says, but we have many more years on earth, God willing, so we'll see."

Haven didn't know whether to be offended or not. So, Naima really didn't fully trust her yet. Well, she could show her better than she could tell her anyway.

Naima continued speaking, "I really think instead of doing a pop up, you should talk to Chris first, you are ready to burst with this baby at any minute, you look like you are about to pop. You shouldn't even be driving, let alone popping up at some chick house for a confrontation."

Tears slowly escaped the corners of Haven's eyes. "All I ever wanted was for someone to love me the same way that Kaden loves you. Why does that seem so impossible?"

"See, there's your problem right there. Don't try and compare your relationship to anyone else. Focus on being happy inside your own relationship on your terms. And did you ever stop to think, that as much as Kaden loves me, it didn't stop him from cheating on me," raising her eyebrow in Haven's direction, "Think about that the next time you go comparing your situation to someone else's.

Wiping her face as she concentrated on driving, Haven had to agree that Naima had a point and what did she look like popping up on someone nine months pregnant anyway?

"Ok, you are making some sense over there. So what do you suggest we do, since you shot down my pop up idea?"

"I don't know, I haven't been to a mall in a while. You think you up to something like that?

"Compared to what I was about to do, a walk through the mall should be a breeze."

"Cool, let's go to Pentagon City since we're already on this side of town or would you prefer Tysons Corner?"

"Let's do Tysons. I want to stop by Louis Vuitton and get a new purse and maybe a baby bag."

"Why do you need a Louis Vuitton baby bag? You're only going to be able to use it for a short amount of time anyway before you know longer need it."

"I know, but it's what I want."

"Alright, I need to get a gift for the baby anyway. So the bag is on me."

"Oh, then we definitely going now." Haven said hopping onto the highway.

"You so crazy." Naima laughed.

Leaving the Louis Vuitton store with her new baby bag and purse, Haven was in a much better mood than when she left the house. Naima was a God send.

"Ok, you got your little bag. Where to now?"

"How about the Cheesecake Factory? I am starving."

"I remember those good ole preggers days. Namiyah wasn't so bad, but Kalani was another story. If I wasn't eating every five minutes, I turned into a demon child. So, to the Cheesecake Factory it is."

Not even seated at the restaurant for a good ten minutes, Haven couldn't believe her eyes. Kicking Naima under the table to get her attention, she nodded in the direction of the bar. Raising her head sharply when she felt the kick, "What in the world?"

"Shh, look who just walked in."

Turning her head slowly to see what had Haven's panties all in a bunch, Naima was shocked to see Emeri and Camille sitting at the bar engaged in animated conversation like life long friends.

Shaking her head as she mumbled, "What are the odds?" Naima was too through.

"I wonder how they know each other."

"Yeah, that seems weird and just weird." Naima added for emphasis.

Getting up as graciously as possible as a full term pregnant woman could, Haven joined Naima on her side of the table to get a better view.

"Look, they're no longer laughing, they seem to be arguing now."

The waiter came over to their table then, "Are you ladies ready to order?"

"Water please." They said in unison without taking their eyes of the two at the bar.

"Would you like to start with an appetizer or salad?"

Haven was beginning to get irritated with the waiter; she just wanted him to go away. Breaking her gaze from the bar she looked him up and down. "We haven't looked at the menu yet. Can you just get our water please?"

"Sure Misss." The waiter huffed and walked away.

Finally, she thought. Turning her head back to face the bar, "Ok, what I miss?"

"Nothing much, they still seem to be arguing."

"Oh. Camille better watch her step, because that bitch Emeri is crazy."

"So, now you want to defend Camille? No more than two seconds ago you wanted to pull a Bonnie and Clyde on her."

"Ha ha, very funny. I don't want to see her die; I just don't want her fucking my husband.

Movement to the side caught Naima's eye, "Speaking of husbands, isn't that Chris right there?"

"What th-"

Haven watched in disbelief as Chris strolled up and kissed Camille on the lips right at the bar for the entire world to see."

Naima knew that any voice of reason was out of the window now. No one knew Haven like she did, and she knew Haven was going to explode, pregnant and all.

"Oh hell nah, it's on now."

Jumping up like a hurdle jumper, and not like someone that was pregnant, Haven was across the restaurant at the bar before Naima could pick up her cane.

"What the fuck are you doing?"

Haven screamed as she smacked Chris across the face and kicked Camille in her knee. Reaching her hand back to slap Chris again, he caught her arm in mid swing. "You need to calm down," he hissed.

"I will not calm down." The other people at the bar had cut off their conversations to watch the scene. Naima saw one of the bartenders signaling security. This is about to get ugly.

"Why the fuck are you at the bar kissing this bitch, when your sorry ass isn't returning any of my calls or coming home at night?"

"You must have lost your mind." Chris replied in a low

menacing voice. "You need to lower your voice and if you attempt to hit me again, they will be taking you out of here on a stretcher. Do you understand?"

Sucking in her breath, Haven spit directly in Chris' eye, "Fuck you."

Releasing her hand to grab a napkin from the bar to wipe the spit out of his eye, Chris was seething. "You are going to regret that." Grabbing Haven by the arm, he practically dragged her out the door of the restaurant.

Naima didn't know what to do, she wanted to give them time to talk and figure things out. Standing directly in front of Camille and Emeri, she decided to address Camille since Emeri was refusing to acknowledge her presence, which was fine, she had no desire to speak with her anyway.

"Camille, how could you?"

"I'm good, thank you and how are you?" she replied.

"I was better before you and Chris were kissing at the bar. How could you do this?"

Shrugging her shoulders, "Why do you care anyway? She's the same 'friend' that was sleeping with your husband. I think it's pathetic that you befriended her again."

"What does that have to do with you and Chris? Who I chose to be friends with is no concern of yours."

"Neither is who I'm kissing at a bar." Camille turned back to face the bar, dismissing Naima.

"Camille, don't turn your back on me."

Turning back to face Naima, "Why are you harassing me? I no longer work for you. I don't owe you anything, especially an explanation. Now if you'll excuse me, I would like to get back to enjoying my dinner which doesn't include you."

Properly chastised, there was nothing for Naima to do but leave. The only problem with that was Haven had driven and who knows where Chris had dragged her off too. Figuring it was a good idea to at least gather their things and look for Haven, she went back to their table to retrieve their purses and also let the waiter, who was just placing their water on the table, know that they would not be returning.

Dragging her into the garage, Chris was finally going to teach Haven a lesson. Who did she think she was causing a scene in the restaurant like that?

"Chris, let me go! I swear I'm going to fuck you up for this!" She screamed.

Throwing her into the back wall of the garage, "You're not going to do shit." He said smacking her across her face with enough force to bust her lip. "Who do you think you are causing a scene?"

Haven was in shock. Who was this person; he'd never hailed off and hit her before. Wiping the blood off her lip, she tried to push away from the wall.

"I'm your wife."

Chris almost laughed in her face at that statement.

"I'm carrying your child, why are you doing this to me?"

In his rage for her acting out in front of Camille, Chris had temporarily forgotten about their baby. "Shit, what was he doing?" He thought.

Trying to calm down and get his emotions in check, he prepared to help Haven up by reaching out a hand to her.

She flinched, scooting down the wall, "If you touch me again, I will tell them that you attempted to rape me and they will put your ass back in jail. And for longer this time because it will be your second offense."

All Chris saw was red as he grabbed her by her throat and began to squeeze the life out of her. He was not going back to jail again for a crime he didn't commit. Haven's eyes were starting to roll back in her head; Chris squeezed harder.

"Hey, what's going on out here?"

Breaking out of his trance, Chris turned to see security racing toward him with a concerned Naima right behind them.

Letting go of Haven's neck, he took off through the door to the exit stairs. If he kept fucking with Haven, that dumb bitch was going to make sure he ended up back in jail.

Making her way to the parking garage behind security at a slower pace, a bad feeling overcame Naima as she saw Chris run into the stairwell. She felt like something tragic had happened or was about to happen. She stopped short when she heard what sounded like gasping noises coming from the far back left side of the garage. Moving as fast as her legs and cane would allow, she saw Haven slumped on the floor in the corner with blood escaping from a gash in her forehead.

"Oh no." Letting go of her cane, falling to her knees to be able to check Haven for body injuries, "Haven, can you hear me?" Naima was frantic. Haven didn't look good at all, in addition to the gash on her forehead, she had finger marks around her neck, her mouth was bloody and two of her teeth were on the ground. Reaching for her purse that she had dropped on the ground, Naima recovered her cell and dialed 9-1-1.

Sitting in the waiting area as the hospital was taking care of Haven, she was visibly shaken. The Doctors' had decided not to take any chances and chose to do an emergency C-section to get the baby out. As a result baby Kadir was doing just fine. She had chosen the name since Haven hadn't been in the frame of mind to do so and no one had seen or heard from Chris since the fiasco at the restaurant. She hoped Haven liked the name. The Doctor said that Haven's wounds weren't as bad as they looked. Granted she would have to get her teeth replaced, but the gash in her head wasn't that deep and she hadn't suffered a tremendous loss of oxygen when she was choked. All in all, she would be fine, emotionally beat up yes, but physically, she would recover.

Dropping her head into her hands, Naima was beat; she wondered if God had heard her prayer tonight. Awakened by the sound of footsteps, she was unaware that she had dozed off. Looking up to see who was approaching her, her heart did a flip flop, as she watched Kaden make his way to her. She was beyond grateful, even if just for tonight, God had answered her prayer; Kaden had come when she needed.

Chapter 9

Interlude

It really pisses me off that Mama still thinks I need a baby sitter. Talking about I'm at that age where all teenage girls made bad decisions about boys. Instead of worrying about boys, she should have been worrying about the man that was in charge of watching me. Things were different now. I was no longer the green twelve-year-old that Mr. CT had first encountered. I am fifteen now and if he wanted the goods, damnit, he was going to have to get used to paying for them. I would be eighteen in three years and I planned on going to college. There was no way my Mama could afford that and even keeping my grades at a 4.0 average, there was no guarantee that I would get a full scholarship from the school of my choice. It was time to take my future into my own hands; Mr. CT was going to be my full paid scholarship. Yes, it's time we turned the tables, time for a new commander-in-chief.

Emeri had Coleen exactly where she wanted her. She was running scared, who would have thought that the haughty Coleen could be brought down a notch. Someone should have taught her long ago that if you lie down with dogs you are bound to catch fleas.

Entering the outpatient therapy clinic Emeri was elated to be meeting with Dr. Tyson Mills again. He was her new therapist and she couldn't have been more thrilled, it had been too long since she had male stimulation in her life. Having signed in at the receptionist desk for her appointment, Emeri sat down to wait for them to call her name. Looking through the magazines on the table, not seeing anything of interest to her, she took to observing the waiting area instead. To her immediate right, there was a young teenage girl with a baby. Emeri wondered why she was here, remembering her own pre-teen and teen years, she could only imagine.

"Emeri Castado, the Doctor will see you now." The receptionist called out. Finally, she thought as she rose to meet the girl at the front who would escort her to Dr. Mills' office. Following the rotund receptionist to his office, she had to slow her pace so she wouldn't run the girl over. Letting her into his office, the receptionist left her alone to wait. Sitting in the chair at the front of his desk, she wasn't alone for two minutes before he entered his office.

"Hello Ms. Castado." He said as he closed the door.

"Hi Dr. Mills."

"Please, this is our second meeting, call me Tyson. I want you to be comfortable. If it's ok with you, I'd like to call you Emeri, so we can have a less formal environment."

"I would like that Tyson."

"Good." Pulling his chair around his desk so he could still

face her without the desk being an obstacle between them, he continued, "How are you today?"

"I'm doing ok."

"Just ok?" he asked while fixating chocolate brown eyes on her light brown ones. She blushed. Horrified that he could make her react to him she broke eye contact. What the hell is wrong with me? No man has ever made me blush before.

"I've been better I guess."

Really?" he asked as he picked up his pen and paper, while cutting the tape recorder on. "Would you care to elaborate? When do you remember life being happier, better?"

Shrugging as she gazed off into the distance. "When my Mama was alive, she always made life better."

"So, is it a safe assumption to say that you've only been happy when your Mother was around?"

"Yeah, I'll agree with that."

"Your mom has been gone for about five years now, correct?"

"Mmmhmmn."

"You haven't been happy since then?"

"Not really."

"You know, happiness is what you make it. No more, no less. If you think happy, you'll be well on the road to being happy."

"It's not that I don't want to be happy, my life has never offered me anything to be happy about."

Something about Emeri touched a place in Tyson's heart. It saddened him to see such a beautiful young woman actually believe that there was no reason for her to be happy.

"Why do you feel that way?"

Interlude

I was officially a college student. I had just registered for my last class and everything was a go. My life was on its way to getting better. Mama had cried her little eyes out when I left, but I had to get away from that place, it was suffocating me. Mr. CT had the nerve to try and see me before I left for school, running up on me in an alley as I walked home from my part-time job one day. When I refused him sexually, he tried to attack me. Too bad for him, it would be the last alley he saw.

Pressed against the wall, gasping for air as his fingers tightened around my throat, my mind wanted to take a leave of absence. I knew if I stopped concentrating on breathing and passed out, this would mark the end of my existence, right here at this spot, in this dirty alley and I refused to have the story of my life end this way. Frantically reaching my hands into the back pocket of my jeans as he continued to squeeze the air from my body, I knew I didn't have much longer before consciousness was lost. Finally, feeling what I was searching for, I made my move quickly. With the blade concealed in my hand, I raised my arm up and dug the tip into the back of his neck with all my might. Yelling in pain, he released one hand from around my throat, to grab the back of his neck, giving me a second to suck air back into my deprived lungs. A second is all the time I needed. Not giving him a chance to continue the assault, I raised the blade masked in my hand, and cut the wrist that was co-conspirator to the hand that was trying, though unsuccessfully now, to cut off my air supply.

With him now withering in pain, it was amusing to see the assaulter now become the assaulted. Taking full advantage of the table turned situation, I was not letting him get away with what he did to me. Blade swinging, I got him to the ground. Straddling him, I proceeded to keep slicing. He moved his hands to cover his face. Little did he know I didn't want his face; I wanted his throat, which was exposed. Walking away from the stilled body, I grinned from ear to ear, mirroring the deep gash the police would find etched in his throat.

Pushing the unfortunate memory out of her mind, Emeri twisted her mouth to the side; she knew she was going to have to talk about Mr. CT sooner or later. She couldn't avoid the topic forever.

"I was sexually abused as a child." She had spoken so softly that Tyson had to lean forward in his chair to hear her.

"Did you ever tell anyone?"

"No, this is my first time mentioning it."

"Why do you think that is?"

"Because I was ashamed of myself for letting it happen."

"Emeri, look at me." Shifting liquefied eyes to his, "There is no reason to be ashamed; this was something that was done to you, not vice versa. You are the innocent in this situation."

Diverting her eyes once again, "I'm ashamed because as I got older, I started to like it. That's not normal."

"On the contrary, it is very normal for an abused person to feel that way. You'd be amazed at how many victims fall in love with their abusers over time and begin to think that they can trust no one but them. Listen to me; you're not the only one that something like this has happened to."

"Then why do I feel as if I'm in a world of one, where no one can understand?"

"Because you've kept this bottled up for so long. I'm going to recommend that you start attending a support group for people that have suffered from sexual abuse, so that you can see that you are most certainly not in a world of one. Would you consider going down to the station and filing a police report about the person that did this to you?"

"There is no need."

"Are you sure? I know it's been a while, but the court system can still make them pay for what they did to you."

"He's dead." Tyson stopped writing when she said that last statement with such finality in her voice.

"Okay. Do you know how he died?"

"Yeah, I killed him."

Ill prepared for Emeri's confession, Tyson was, for the first time in his career at a loss for words. He had never suffered abuse. His own family had been a nurturing and loving one. Considering the notes that he had read in Emeri's file, he knew she was pretty messed up, mainly because she hadn't grown up with the father that she had yearned for, but he had no idea that another big reason stemmed from sexual abuse as a child. Put in her position, he didn't really blame her for killing her abuser. He probably would have done the same if the opportunity presented itself.

"Did that shock you? You've read my file, they say I'm crazy, you shouldn't be surprised."

"I don't think you're crazy. Sad, angry and misguided. Yes. Crazy? No."

"Really? Twelve jurors and a judge would argue otherwise."

"They don't know the whole story. I believe you can turn your life around if you really want to, if you focused on wanting to be happy and not let your past destroy your present."

"How would I do that?"

"For starters, this feud that you have going with your half sister, why not end it?"

"Because, Naima grew up with everything, she got the father I always wanted. If I had had a father around, no one would have been able to abuse me. I would have had someone there to protect me."

"Why do you blame Naima for you growing up without a father? Did it ever occur to you maybe she wanted a sister and felt just as robbed of the opportunity as you feel robbed of growing up without a father?"

"I don't care whose fault it is. She should have to pay."

"Did you ever stop to think that maybe the person you're really angry at is your mother?"

Emeri was surprised when she felt moisture behind her lids. Talking about her Mama always made her break down.

"I can't blame her. She's not here to defend herself."

"In your process to not blame her, you're lashing out at everyone else for something they had no control over." Softening his voice, Tyson put his pen and paper down to focus all of his attention on Emeri. "Think about it, what would you say to your mother if she were here?"

"I would ask her how could she do this too me." Tears free falling now, Emeri didn't care if Tyson saw them or not, "I would tell her she fucked up my whole life, but I still love her and I need her here with me now." Turning to bury her head into Tyson's chest, "why did she leave me? I need her, I need her..." Her voice trailed off.

Somewhat expecting the tirade, Tyson was excited that Emeri

had finally made a break through. He knew after speaking with her previous therapist Coleen, that she seemed to be in a state of denial. He wondered if it was harder for Emeri to confide in Coleen because she was a woman.

Camille could not believe the way Chris treated Haven the day they all ran into one another at the Cheesecake Factory. It was one thing for him to be sticking through the marriage until he got what he wanted, but assault and battery of his wife in her advanced stage of pregnancy was beyond comprehensible to her.

She never wanted to see anything bad happen to the baby and was surprised that Chris would go to such extremes with Haven in a public place and risk hurting the baby he was so excited she was carrying. The whole situation just didn't make sense and before things got more out of hand, she needed answers. Since the incident at the restaurant, Chris had been staying with her trying to lay low. He hadn't been to see the baby yet, didn't even know the baby's name and anytime she brought up the situation he would say it wasn't up for discussion. Well his self pity grace period was over. Today was "D" day and she was coming to collect the answers she sought. Walking into the garage, where Chris was fixing the brakes on his car, she figured she could talk to him now.

"Chris."

"What?"

"Please use manners and don't speak to me that way." Huffing as he looked up at Camille, Chris could tell she was going to have her say, but that didn't mean he had to make it easy for her.

"What, can I help you with? Is that better?"

"Somewhat." Turning a bucket over to sit on she faced him as half his body was under the car. "I want to talk about the other night. Don't you think you owe it to me to explain what happened?"

"Not really." He replied. Not even bothering to pause in what he was doing,

"Well, I think that you do. So we will be discussing right now."

"Fine Camille, whatever you say. What do you want to hear from me? That I messed up? Ok," he threw down one of the tools he was using causing a loud clanking noise, and picked up another, "I messed up."

"I just don't understand why you got so mad at her. You acted like she didn't have a right to say anything to you in there."

"She doesn't have rights to say anything that has to do with me, are we clear on that?"

"Don't use that tone with me. All I'm saying is you didn't have to react that way. And furthermore, I thought you were excited about the baby? Why would you intentionally hurt Haven knowing that the baby's life could be at stake? None of your actions from that night make any kind of sense to me and I need an explanation."

Chris had to hand it to Camille, she was no pushover, she had come out here to get answers and that is what she fully expected to do. People could underestimate her if they wanted to, but he knew better.

"Honestly, I lost my head a little that night. I never meant for things to go as far as they did. That's why I haven't been home or to see the baby. For all I know, she could have the police waiting for me when I get there."

"I seriously doubt she will have the police waiting for you. I'm pretty sure Haven is smart enough to realize if you haven't been at home, then chances are you must be staying with me. She could have sent them over here at any time, but she didn't. You know Haven loves you, and she probably still feels guilty for what she made you go through years ago. She's not going to put you behind bars again. Trust me."

"Why are you defending her?"

"I'm not defending her; I'm trying to help you to stop being stuck up your own ass for once and go see your child. I know it's killing you to not know what he looks like, or his name. Everything you missed with Kaven, you have the opportunity to witness with this baby. Stop making excuses and go."

"Will you come with me?"

"Ok, see now you have gone and bumped your head. I am not showing up at you and your wife's doorstep, with her husband in tow." Camille threw her hands up in the air not believing his nerve. "Sorry Busta, you will have to do this alone. I will not disrespect her house, where her children are."

"I don't know about this."

"Why not try calling first? See what she's willing and not willing to do."

Pondering for a moment as he secured the last brake pad in place, Chris figured that Camille had a point.

"Kadir is absolutely beautiful." Naima couldn't help admiring his little fingers and toes. He smelled like baby powder and Johnson and Johnson's baby lotion, just yummy. Her heart melted, just like it did every time she was around children, whether they be hers or someone else's. He was staring up at her with beautiful bright green eyes.

"Please explain to me how both of your babies got green eyes? Usually one will get them and the other won't. Like my kids. Green eyes completely skipped Kalani…he has hazel ones like his Momma though! But girl, there is no way Chris can deny these children."

Haven was trying to focus on whatever Naima was going on and on about, but for the life of her, she just couldn't. A month had passed since Kadir's birth, a month since that crazy night when Chris put her in the hospital. A month and he still hadn't seen or held his baby.

"Yeah, it is crazy how much he looks like Chris. Kaven, looks more like me and still miraculously came out with those green eyes. Guess in my case eye color is not the dominant gene."

Concerned with her lack of enthusiasm, Naima stopped doting on Kadir to give Haven her full attention. "You ok over there? You seem a little out of it."

Haven shrugged her shoulders, "I'm ok I guess. It's just hard for me to belie--" interrupted by the shrill sound of the phone, "I haven't heard from Chris." She said, finishing her statement.

"Hello." She answered into the receiver.

There was a prolonged silence before she softly heard her name spoken at the other end. Gesturing at Naima to get her attention while she pointed to the phone and mouthed, "Speak of the Devil."

"Hello." She repeated into the receiver, as if she hadn't heard them speak the first time.

"Haven, it's me."

"Who is me?"

"Please don't play games. You know who this is. Can you

stop this and listen to what I have to say for a minute?"

"Why should I?"

"Because I want to apologize."

Haven broke into a fit of laughter, the nerve of this guy. "You wait a whole month to apologize? You haven't seen your son, you're pathetic."

"Damn, could you stop being difficult and just listen to me for a second?"

"Ohhhh, so now I'm difficult? You're the one that tackled me in a parking lot garage. Did you forget about that? Or how about you trolluping around with that little bitch Camille out in the open for the entire world to see? You're the one that didn't come to the hospital to your son when he was born and you're the one who has been God only knows where for the past month, then you have the nerve to call out of the blue with a phone call apology, no flowers, no candy, asking me to listen to your trifling ass. And I'm the one who's difficult? Please!"

"You taking things too far as you usually do, which seems to be the Haven way. All I want to do is see my son. Is it clear for me to do that?"

"What do you mean is it clear?" and it suddenly dawned on her, Chris was afraid she would have the police waiting for his ass when he got there. Humph, he deserved no less than that, with his wanna be Ike Turner ass. But she didn't feel it was fair strictly because she shouldn't have sent him to jail years ago, serving time for a crime he never committed.

Sighing in defeat, "It's clear, feel free to come and visit your son. But if you bring that whore Camille anywhere near my house all bets are off and it will not be clear for you, the boys in blue will haul your lying, cheating, abusive ass away kicking and screaming for all I care."

"Aight, you made your point. Chill out ok. Is it cool to come now? I can be there in about ten."

"Now is fine."

"Thanks, I really appreciate this."

"Whatever. Get off my phone." She hung up.

"So," Naima chimed in, "I take it he's on his way over?"

"Yeah, I would really appreciate it if you stayed till he's done visiting Kadir. I don't trust him not to try and attack me again."

"I don't think Chris is that crazy."

"You don't know him like I do. He is on get back. That night at the restaurant all but proves it."

"Well, when you put it that way, I'm inclined to believe you. Cause that night was crazy. I still can't believe that he and Camille have a fling going. She was always such a sweet girl. I wonder how that came about anyway. What are you going to do?" Naima asked as she placed kisses all over Kadir's fat cheeks.

"I haven't decided yet. I don't know what to do."

"Have you ever considered praying about it and letting God lead you from there? That's what I did when we were going through our situation. I prayed till I didn't know what else to do, then I prayed some more. He knew exactly what to do and we're friends now because of me praying so much."

"I prayed about the Chris situation and look where that got my ass."

"Maybe you weren't praying for the right thing." Walking across the room to place Kadir in his bassinet, Naima went back over to Haven and grabbed her hand. "How about we pray together? I will lead this one off and over time you'll get more comfortable and you can lead."

Dropping to their knees on the carpet, they clenched hands and Naima began, "Lord, we come to you humbly in search of guidance and strength. I pray that Haven and Chris seek you in any and all decisions they make moving forward with their marriage. Lord only you know what the future holds for the two of them as they work on rebuilding their marriage and raising the two beautiful sons you have entrusted into their care in this world. Please lead them in the way that they should go and grant peace and serenity to deal with any decisions that they make from this moment on. In your name we pray, Amen." As they were rising to their feet at the end of the prayer, the doorbell rang. Chris had arrived.

Chapter 10

Damir sat at his desk with coffee in hand about to launch his internet research on Kaden. He'd officially decided he wanted Naima to himself, which meant he had to go through the process of eliminating him from her life and step one was finding a reason to fire him. No woman wanted a man that was unemployed. Pulling up Google's search engine, he typed in Kaden's full name and waited for the results to load on the page. The first link he saw was for Kaden's Wikipedia Bio, he could care less where he was born and that nonsense, the second link was of some tabloid scandal that took place years ago. The third link was the one that piqued his interest; it contained information about an accident that had taken place some years back. Clicking the link, he vaguely remembered when he met Kaden him mentioning something about an accident, or he should say "the" accident that ended his football career.

Practically spilling his coffee over his keyboard, Damir placed the cup down with a heavy force. He was shocked by what he read on the monitor. The place where Kaden's accident occurred was the same place his sister Alanna was when she was in the car accident that took her life. Eyes steadily roaming the article, Damir found what he was looking for, the date. Either this was one wild and crazy coincidence or the two of them were in the same accident.

Taking a quick scan of his office, framed photos of he and Alanna lined his desk and walls. He couldn't count the number of times Kaden had been in his office during his employment and not once had he ever mentioned anything about her. Swiftly jumping out of his chair, Damir left his office heading for Kaden's cube. He demanded answers and he demanded them now.

"That will be perfect." Kaden said as he ended the phone call. He smiled to himself. Everything was almost in place and he couldn't be more pleased. So into his own thoughts, he didn't see Damir enter his cube until he was almost directly on top of him. Already feeling a certain type of way about Damir, his unexpected intrusion into his space was very unwelcomed. It was less about Damir as a person and more about the way this nicca looked at his wife. He could see it in his eyes the day he stopped by to visit Naima. He knew his wife was a beautiful woman, even more so now because of her ability to not give up. He was proud of the way she never complained about anything and took everything in stride and kept it moving.

Shoving a picture in his face, "Do you know this girl?" Damir said in a terse tone.

Rising to a standing position, Kaden had to put Damir in his place. "Aye, before you stroll into my area with that tone, you need to address me another way," Staring him straight into his eyes, "and never shove anything into my face again."

Damir's temper escalated at Kaden's stance. "Don't talk to

me that way muthafucka, I'm the reason you have this job, did you forget? You better take care to remember that."

Not flinching, "You heard what I said. Don't you forget." Kaden knew a bitch ass nicca when he saw one and he definitely had one swimming in "bitchassness" standing in front of him. "Are we done here?"

Trying to regain his composure Damir was pissed off. So, Kaden thought he was untouchable did he? Every man had a soft spot and everyone knew Naima was his, too bad for this nicca Kaden; his soft spot had been sucked, kissed, bitten and fucked by him. Wonder what his "untouchable" ass would say about that, but now wasn't the time to break up his world...but soon.

Forcing himself to calm down, Damir handed the photo to Kaden this time, "Do you recognize this girl?"

Looking down at the picture Damir had given him, Kaden saw the girl and handed the photo back. "Yeah, I met her in Texas."

"You know she's my sister, you never felt the need to tell me you knew her?"

Shrugging his shoulders, "What was there to say? I've seen the photos in your office; I know she's your sister, what would you gain by knowing that we had met one another in a previous life?" Waving him off, "Who cares?"

"I care." Damir was seething, "I was reading your file online and I'm willing to bet the two of you were involved in the same accident back then."

Returning to his seated position behind his desk, trying to make Damir get the hint, "Didn't your parents teach you not to believe everything you read?"

"It's true muthafucka, you were there. You saw my sister

when she died." Damir was yelling now, causing a disturbance in the office. People were starting to turn and stare.

Feeling an impending threat, Kaden rose back to his feet.

"What if I did? It wasn't my fault and there's nothing to be done about it now. It's over."

"Fuck you!" Damir screamed lunging at him, forget about his world now, "that's why I fucked your wife!"

Kaden felt the impact of his words more than the one from his body. Moving swiftly to deflect the blows coming his way, he spun Damir into a headlock.

"You know, I've been staying off your ass because you were my boss, but fuck you and this job. As for your sister Alanna, or better known as 'Apple', yeah I fucked the diseased whore; she damn near ruined my life. Actually she did. Meeting her was the worst thing that ever happened to me. I would probably still have my career if I never fucked with her ass." Squeezing his arms around Damir's neck a little harder for added emphasis, "Now take that shit to your grave. As for my wife, if I were you, I wouldn't contact her again or you may be seeing your sister sooner than you think."

Abruptly letting Damir go letting him fall to the ground, Kaden grabbed the few things he kept at his desk, stepped over Damir who was laid out on the ground trying to catch his breath and headed out of the building. He needed to speak with his wife.

Naima was enjoying her first day back at work. She'd finally stopped avoiding the place and came in, since she could move around a little more freely with her cane, she felt like she could move mountains. She had no idea how much she missed work until she stepped back into her office. Everything was exactly as she had left it. Looking at the photos of Namiyah and Kalani when they were younger brought a smile to her face. She and Kaden really did have some gorgeous kids and so what if she was biased. She was their Momma that gave her the right.

Sitting at her desk hearing the children's laughter as they ran around outside kept Naima's smile intact, soon she would be able to run around the yard with Kalani and she was so excited she couldn't stand herself.

"God thank you so much for blessing me. Things could have turned out a completely different way. You're awesome. Amen" she shot a quick prayer to the Man above. Talking to Him numerous times a day kept her sane.

"Mrs. Fairchild," the receptionist buzzed in, "your husband is on his way to your office.

No sooner had she received the heads up when Kaden walked through her office door.

"Hi Baby, this is a nice surprise on my first day back." She slowly rose to her feet in anticipation for his kiss, a kiss that was not forthcoming today.

"We need to talk." Kaden said without a trace of kindness in his voice as he closed the door.

Oh oh, Naima thought, something bad must have happened.

"What's wrong?"

"You tell me. I got fired….quit my job. However you decide to look at it."

"What! Why?"

"You mean besides assault? Damir figured out I knew Alanna, but that wasn't the kicker," Walking over to where she stood at her desk with tears in his eyes, "the kicker was finding out my wife has been fucking my boss."

The color drained out of Naima's face. Damir had told Kaden about their one night together after all this time, or she wondered if he told him about when they were dating back in the day as well? She was banking on just the last time he knew about, she hoped that she was right.

"Baby, let me explain."

"There's no need, I don't want to hear about it. I already forgave you."

"Well, I am going to tell you anyway." She felt she had to plead her case. "You haven't been home lately and I felt neglected. It was only that one night; I got caught up in a weak moment." Sticking out her bottom lip, pouting, "You're never around anymore and when you are you don't want to be bothered, are you cheating on me?"

Coming around her desk, emerald green eyes collided with wet hazel ones, putting his hand under her chin, "Mocha, how could you think that? I haven't touched another woman since you let me back into your life and I never will. I love you. Don't you know that by now? If you had doubts why didn't you come and ask me?"

Face completely drenched in tears now, Naima was ashamed of herself, she and Kaden had already overcome so much.

"Because I didn't want to hear you say yes."

"Mocha, the reason I have been so busy is because I have something big in the works. I can't tell you what it is now, but I want it to be a surprise. You've been such a trooper through this whole experience and I want to show you how much I love you. You're superwoman to me."

He had effectively succeeded in making her feel like a bigger jerk than she already felt.

"Kaden, I'm sorry. I didn't mean it, it meant nothing to me."

"I forgive you baby, how could I not? You've forgiven me for much worse, but from now on Mocha we have to talk about things that are bothering us. If something looks suspicious just ask me. I'm in this for the long haul. It will always be you and I tell the end. That's where it all started right?" Brushing his fingers lightly over her cheek, he fell in love with her all over again. She was his and no one would ever break them apart.

"Ma, can I talk to you for a minute?"

Pushing the papers that she was reading to the side, Naima more than welcomed the distraction. "Sure Muffin, what's on your mind?"

Sitting on the bed next to her mom, Namiyah laid her head in her lap.

"I've been doing some thinking after our talk about you and Aunt Emeri's situation." Waiting for her to get situated Naima waited patiently for her to continue. "And I've come to the conclusion that I hate her. I know you say it's not right to hate people, but the thought of her being a part of our family disgusts me."

At this point, Naima didn't know what to say about the situation to Namiyah. Granted she didn't find it acceptable to hate anyone but on the other hand, Namiyah was fifteen and temperamental, always had been and probably always would be. She couldn't change her child's way of thinking, all she could do was guide it to the best of her ability.

"Well Muff, you do know how I feel about the word hate, I know your Aunt has done some terrible things and doesn't seem to learn from her mistakes, but it's not our place to judge. Only God can do that, we discussed this, remember? Don't you think I'm angry with her too? At one point, my anger for her was consuming my life. I had to place God on speed dial to get me through many moments from the incident, till now." Pulling Namiyah's head up off her lap forcing her to look at her face to face, "And you see I don't hate her. You'll forgive her in your own time, don't feel you have to rush it, but if you pray for it, it will come."

"She has to pay for what she did to you. She has to." The tears streaking down Namiyah's face were enough to break any mother's heart. Her baby girl was tormented and she didn't know how to help her. Namiyah's hatred for Emeri was consuming her and she was entirely to young to be burdened down like this.

"How would you feel about seeing a counselor? Someone you could talk to, to get your real true feelings out into the open?"

"You mean a therapist like Aunt Emeri goes to? Ma, there is nothing wrong with me; I don't want to see a therapist."

Naima placed a kiss on her forehead, "Think about it ok? Now go get your shower and get ready for bed. I'll be in to say good night in a few."

"Kay. I love you."

"Love you too Muffin."

Lying back on the bed, no longer interested in the papers she had been reading, Naima prayed for God to give her baby peace. Reaching for the phone on the night stand, she called the one person that would know what to do.

"There's my baby, I just had you on my mind."

Grinning as her spirits were instantly lifted, her mom was the best mood pick me up God ever created.

"Well hello to you too, how did you know it was me?"

"Chile, you know I keep caller id in full effect. Never know who will come calling here these days. How's my baby?"

"I'm ok; it's been a long day."

"Your Momma could tell honey, probably why you've been on my mind. Want to talk about it?"

"Yes, I need to talk about it." Taking a deep breath before continuing, "Namiyah just announced to me that she hates Emeri. She's allowing her hate to consume her and I have no idea what to do. Mainly because I struggle with my own emotions about Emeri, but I want to teach Namiyah to do what's right."

"Well baby, we have all choked and burned where your sister is concerned and Namiyah is entitled to her emotions, they are something you cannot control. All you can do is be there for her and pray God can heal our family as a unit."

"I know Ma, but I think she needs more. You know that girl has a temper on her. I recommended counseling, what do you think?"

"That may be a good idea baby. What about that Coleen woman? Your Dad was fond of her even though she and Emeri didn't hit it off, maybe she will be good for Namiyah."

"Momma you are a life saver! That is an excellent idea, especially since Coleen is already familiar with our crazy situation. Can you have Daddy send me her information? I think Coleen and Namiyah will hit it off nicely."

"I'll have your Dad send the information over first thing in the morning. Everything else going ok?

"Yes Ma'am. Everything is wonderful."

"Ok Chile. Well you go on and tend to that family of yours, while I clean up before bed."

"Love you."

"Love you too. Night."

Smiling as she hung up the phone, she couldn't help thinking how much she loved her mom.

"Hello Namiyah, how are you today?"

"Upset."

"Why are you upset?"

"Because, I told my mom that I did not want to see a therapist and she made me come anyway."

"I can see how being made to do something you don't want to do could upset you. Your mom is worried about you that's all." Shifting in a seat, "How about instead of therapy, we call this a friendly chat with two individuals and go from there?"

"I guess that would be alright."

"Good." Coleen was happy for that one small victory. Sensing that she was on shaky ground with Namiyah, she had to tread lightly. She honestly thought the direct approach would be better suited with her. Namiyah was very bright and didn't seem like the type to play typical teenage games.

"Do you want to jump right in and talk about your Aunt Emeri? Or is there something else you would like us to chat about first?"

"We can talk about Emeri, I don't mind." She said quietly.

"What seems to be the problem?" Coleen sat back and waited for Namiyah to begin. She wouldn't rush her, not that Namiyah seemed like the type to be rushed anyway. She would go at her own pace.

"I hate her." She stated plainly, "I don't think I have a problem. I think that Emeri has a problem, or you could say she is the problem. My mom doesn't think hate is acceptable, which brings me here to you."

"Why do you hate her?"

Tears suddenly appeared in Namiyah's eyes, "Because she almost killed my mom."

"Do you think she intended too?"

"Mommy says she know she didn't, but whether she intended to or not, she almost did. If it weren't for her none of this would have happened in the first place. Like I learned in Chemistry class for every action, there is a reaction."

"Is that what you are doing? Reacting?"

"Yes. That's exactly what I'm doing."

"What do you hope or think hating her will accomplish? Do you think it affects her in any way?"

Namiyah stopped to think. She hadn't thought about it like that before. Hating her Aunt was affecting her more than it affected Emeri, but she still had to pay for what she had done.

"When you put it like that, I guess my hating her will accomplish nothing except continually pissing me off."

"You're a very intelligent girl; look at all we've covered already. What do you think it will take for you to forgive her?

"It would take my mom never being hurt in the first place and since that's something that cannot be undone," Namiyah's green eyes met Coleen's, "I will never forgive her."

Coleen felt a chill go down her spine at Namiyah's admission.

"You just finished saying how hating Emeri wouldn't accomplish anything, yet you're basically telling me there is no room in your heart to forgive her?

"That is what I'm saying. What's done is done."

Observing Namiyah as she spoke, Coleen couldn't help but see the comparison between her and the Aunt she despised. In some respects, they were just alike. Both strong willed and determined to have their way with hot tempers to add icing to the cake. The one visible difference between the two was Namiyah had a heart; she could still be saved.

Moving out of her chair to kneel in front of Namiyah, "Namiyah, I want us to be friends. How do you feel about that?"

"You're an adult that my mom is paying to have "friendly chats" with me. We can't be friends, because I don't trust you."

For her to only be fifteen, Coleen felt like she was speaking with a grown woman.

"Fair enough. Believe it or not, our chats are strictly confidential. Nothing you say in here will get back to your mother. Everything said in here stays between you and me."

That seemed to have gotten her attention. "Really?"

"Yes, really."

"Cool. Can I ask you a question?"

"Sure. You can ask me anything."

"Is that your son in the photo on your desk?"

Glancing over at her desk at the photo of her and her son Justin, Coleen smiled, "Yes, that's my little monster. He's three."

"He's so cute."

Laughing she replied to Namiyah. "Don't let the cuteness fool you, he can be a terror."

"He reminds me of when my brother Kalani was that little. They have a similar smile."

Coleen could feel her throat closing in on her. She had to

relax. There was no way Namiyah could know anything she was just being inquisitive.

"What a coincidence. Well Ms. Namiyah," she said her name to divert her attention away from the photo, "Our time is up for today. Will you be coming back to see me?"

Namiyah shrugged, "I guess so. It makes my mom happy to know I'm talking to someone, so I'll come to keep her happy." Grabbing her belongings, "I'll see you next week."

"Ok sweetie, see you then."

Coleen sighed with relief as Namiyah shut her office door. Picking the photo of her and Justin up off her desk, she decided it would probably be best if she removed it when Namiyah had her sessions. No point in stirring up the pot, things had been going great with her and Justin's Dad for the past four years and she wanted them to stay that way.

Chapter 11

"What the fu-" Camille mumbled to herself as she sorted through her mail. If Coleen sent her one more 'scared straight' note, about Emeri she was going to have a fit and the two of them would have some serious issues. It not that she didn't love her sister, Coleen could just be so extra sometimes. Always minding business that wasn't hers. She had her own mess to deal with, so it was really in her best interest to mind her business.

Picking up the phone, she dialed Coleen's number.

"Hello."

"Can you please stop mailing these Emeri hate letters to my house? You starting to get on my nerves."

"Well excuse me for being concerned about my baby sister. I do it out of love, I don't want to see anything bad happen to you."

"Nothing bad will happen, stop worrying all your life." Camille cracked a smile, "and I love you too. But, you have to stop looking at me as if I'm a baby. I'm all grown up now sis. Embrace it, love it."

Coleen laughed on the other end.

"Ok, ok. You've made your point. It won't stop me from worrying, but I will send no more warnings through the mail." She paused, "I'll start using email instead."

Camille shook her head at that, some things would never change and Coleen imposing on her life was one of them.

"When are you coming over? I want to see my nephew. I miss my handsome baby."

"I was getting us all packed up before my new and improved 'all grown up' sister called me giving me a lecture about interfering in her life." she said with a smile.

"True. Well, you get the point now. Come on over, we need bonding time."

"You so silly. Me and Justin will be on our way in abut thirty."

"Ok. See you in a little bit."

Racing out to the car when Coleen pulled up, Camille could see through the window that Justin was all smiles. Opening the door to remove him from his car seat, she didn't know who was more excited, him or her.

"Auntie Cam." He said clapping his hands together.

"Jay Jay."

Looking at them in disgust, "Ya'll need to stop. Acting as if you haven't seen each other in years. We were just over here last week." Coleen said.

"A week is way too long." Camille replied as she hugged Justin tighter. Noticing all the stuff Coleen had in the car, she was baffled.

"I mean, are you moving in? What is all this crap?"

Laughing softly, "Girl hush. I didn't know how long we

would be here so I brought some stuff for Jay."

"Yeah, like his whole room."

"Whatever Camille." She said still laughing. "Did you cook us lunch?"

"You know it! Can't have my nephew starving. Who knows what you be feeding this child at home." Camille poked Justin in the stomach, "if you feed him at all, look at him all skin and bones." She tickled him under his chin to which he went into an uncontrollable fit of laughter.

Hitting her on the arm playfully, "My baby is not skin and bones. Hush your mouth. His Daddy would kill me if I starved that child."

Walking to the deck where Camille had set up for lunch, "How is his Dad and that whole situation coming a long?"

Sitting in a deck chair, pouring herself a glass of lemonade from the pitcher Camille had on the table, Coleen thought of the best way to respond to her question.

"It's coming along as best as can be expected. I already know he's not going to leave his wife. I know it was stupid to get involved with a married man, but I was drawn to him, still am. Things aren't the same for him at home he tells me. He seems confused and lost, so I play my roll, counsel him and just be there. I think that's what he appreciates the most. We never argue or anything."

"He doesn't need to argue with you. He has a wife at home to do that with."

"He doesn't argue with her either."

Camille shrugged, "Well if it works for you, it works for me."

"How is Chris?"

Without missing a beat, "Selfish."

"I told you that day one."

"Please save me the free therapy session. If I want one, I'll pay you."

"Ooo, touchy, touchy. New baby at home means Ms. Kitty is probably meowing from neglect."

Camille had to laugh at that, "Will you shut your mouth. You're crazy," Continuing after a spilt second, "You're right though, Ms. Kitty is in need of some attention."

"You have two people to choose from, what's the problem? Even though I can't stand the girl, how is Emeri?"

"She's good I guess. She hasn't really been hanging out with me as much lately. I think she's dating someone."

Coleen was honestly shocked; "Who in their right mind would date that psycho girl?" she quickly amended, "except for you, no offense."

"First off, we never dated. We are just friends."

Coleen snorted, "Friends that make each others kittiess purr. You are not fooling anybody speaking that nonsense."

Rolling her eyes, "Anyway, either way we keep it open for everyone to do their own thing. She's really private, so I don't know who it is, just that someone is in the picture. She seems different."

"Different how?"

"I don't know, nicer I guess. She doesn't seem as crazy."

"For the life of me, I could never understand your attraction to her."

"I like her free spirit."

"Her free psychotic spirit."

"Ok Ms. 'Prim and Proper', since you're so perfect, how

:07

you get caught up with Jay's Dad? Explain that Ms. 'I'm so professional and I don't do anything wrong'.

"I already told you, I was drawn to him. It just happened."

"Now come on Doctor, aren't you the main one telling your patients nothing just happens?"

"Ok, alright you got me. I thought he was sexy, I wanted him, he wanted me and there you have it. You happy now?"

"Well, well the good ol Doc finally comes clean. Will wonders never cease?"

"He's going to stop by and pick up Jay in a little bit. I hope that's ok."

"You know it's not a problem. What may be a problem though, is Emeri knows who Justin's Dad is."

"Yeah, I figured that out the day she threatened me in my office. Why you telling your girl my business? You know I can lose my license over this."

"It slipped out one night and what do you mean she threatened you? You never told me that."

"That's why I don't counsel her anymore."

"I though you did that because of the situation with Jay's Dad, I had no idea it was because she was threatening you."

"Yeah, I told you that girl is psycho. See why I want you to stay away from her?"

"Oh, don't worry sister dear. She's not more psycho than I am and this will be taken care of, I can guarantee it. Don't you worry at all."

Damir was officially off the hook, Emeri decided. She was done with him now. His appeal was gone since Naima no longer entertained him, what was the point. On to the next, as far as she was concerned and sexy ass Tyson was definitely a great next to move on too. He was like nothing she had ever experienced before. Tyson knew about her past and didn't seem too phased by it, he was willing to break the rules for her. They both knew he was putting his job in jeopardy by dating her, yet the courtship continued. The only downfall to him was he kept pushing for reconciliation between she and Naima. As far as Emeri was concerned, there was nothing to reconcile. She and Naima had never had a relationship. The only reason Emeri tolerated Tyson's constant nagging about it was because she did love Ma Cyn and she knew that Ma Cyn would absolutely love it if they could all get along. That would be the only reason, cause lord knows her father, Kenneth, was just like every other man in the world, selfish; every man that is, except Tyson.

Standing at a cool 6 feet even, bowlegged with toffee colored skin, hazelnut brown eyes, soft kiss me lips and the sexiest two moles on his left cheek, he was adorable. It was just not possible for a yummier man to exist.

"Chile, what are you over there thinking about. You're glowing."

Thoughts interrupted by Ma Cyn as she entered the room, Emeri smiled, "Tyson." She answered before thinking.

"Tyson huh? As in your therapist? Why would you be thinking about him?"

Realizing her mistake, she had to think of a quick and adequate answer for Ma Cyn.

"No reason in particular. Our sessions have been going really well. That's all."

"Glad that you finally have someone you feel you can talk to."

"I feel like I can talk to you."

"Of course you can and I'm always here to listen."

"Why don't you hate me?" Emeri asked softly. She had no idea why she had blurted that question out. She could tell Ma Cyn was caught off guard, she was speechless even and that rarely happened to her.

"God never granted me a spirit of hatred," she finally said, "to which I am grateful."

"How could you not?" I almost killed your daughter. Whether I meant to or not, I almost did."

Coming over to sit next to Emeri, Ma Cyn pulled her into a hug.

"I never hated you even then. I prayed that God would look out for you and Naima and he did just that. You're just misguided and hurt. Nothing a loving family and a gold old-fashioned whipping can't cure.

Emeri had to laugh at that. A good old-fashioned whipping, her own Mama had never hit her. She could not imagine going through something like that.

Returning Ma Cyn's hug, Emeri could honestly say that she loved her.

"While we're talking," Ma Cyn began as she pulled out of their hug and sat in a chair on the other side of the room, "this thing with you and Naima needs to stop. I've tried to stay out of it hoping you two could be adults and work through this, but now Namiyah is suffering and I can't have that. She's too young to be going through so much."

Emeri almost bulked at that. In her opinion, Namiyah had it pretty easy. At Namiyah's age Emeri was fighting off a grown man's sexual advances. What was Namiyah fighting, besides hating her? That was something that she could survive.

"Emeri, are you listening?"

Damn, had she zoned out? "Yes, I'm listening."

"Good because it's time for us to have some one on one time. Explain to me why you seem to have it out for Naima. This situation is killing her and I'm trying to understand it myself."

Clearing her throat to stall for time, Emeri tried to think of a reasonable answer, "I don't have it out for Naima per se. I just, I just...." She was at a loss for words. How was she supposed to explain to Ma Cyn that she simply hated that Naima had been the one to have such a good life.

"You're jealous."

"What?!"

"You heard me Chile, I said "jealous" and don't "what" me again."

"Yes, Ma'am." Damn, Emeri thought, Ma Cyn made her feel about Namiyah's age.

"Now, I understand that your father wasn't around while you were growing up, but we're all here now trying to be here for you. You're the one that doesn't seem to be trying."

Head bowed down towards the table, Emeri was embarrassed. She knew that tears would fall soon.

"Why should I have too? I was the one wronged in the situation."

"Emeri, you need to humble yourself. We were all wronged by this situation and you're not making it easier on anyone acting the way that you've been acting. What do you want to see happen inside this family, so we can all finally have some peace?"

"I don't know. I guess I want those years I missed with my Dad back."

"Chile, if we had the power to go back in time, we all would. Unfortunately we cannot, we have to make the most of right now. Your Dad is here, when have you taken the time out for the two of you to strengthen that relationship. He wants to and you want to, so what's the problem?"

Emeri thought about that. What was the problem? Why hadn't she gone out to spend some time with the father she had waited all her life to have? Maybe because deep down she knew he was a liar.

"I really don't know Ma Cyn. I guess I was waiting for him to ask me."

Shaking her head to the heavens, "Lordie, you are your father's child alright. You both are stubborn. He's outside working on the lawn mower. Why not go out there and keep him company? I'm sure he would love that."

"Ok," Emeri said getting out of her seat to place a kiss on Ma Cyn's cheek. I'll go see what he's up too. Thanks for the talk."

"No problem Chile. You think about what I said about you and Naima's situation as well. Ya'll work this thing out." She said looking Emeri directly in the eye.

Taking a slow deep breath so Ma Cyn wouldn't see, "I'll give it some serious thought" Emeri said as she slid out the side door in search of her Dad.

Watching Kenneth sitting on the ground with bits and pieces of the lawn mower spread out all around him, Emeri's emotions were all over the place.

With tears in her eyes she watched the man who was her father pick over his tools. No wonder she was all screwed up when it came to men. She'd been sexually abused as a child, her Dad had been absent from her life, and a new development, he was also a liar. As much as she enjoyed her time with Tyson, she knew it was only a matter of time before he fucked up as well.

"Hi Daddy. Need some help?"

Startled by the sound of her voice, Kenneth looked up from what he was doing.

"Hey Baby. Sure, you can help an old man out. Come on over her and sort through these tools for me so I can attempt to fix this mower."

"Ok." Sitting on the ground next to him, she had no idea what she was looking at. Tools were everywhere. "What am I supposed to look for?"

"Can you hand me a wrench?"

"Sure."

Taking the wrench out of her extended hand he asked, "So, what brings you out here? I know you don't really want to help put a lawn mower back together."

"I just wanted to spend some time with you."

"Really?" He sounded shocked.

Emeri smiled, "Yes, really. I've been thinking maybe we could call a truce. I know it's not your fault that you weren't around to watch me grow up; it's so much easier to blame you because Mama isn't here to blame."

"What brought about this change of heart?"

"Tyson. He's been a huge help to me. Those therapy session are really paying off."

"I'm happy to hear that. Even happier for you. You seem like you're doing better.:

"I am, I'm doing a lot better."

"I can tell. How are things coming along with you and Naima?"

Playing with the tools around them so she wouldn't have to look at him, "Umm they're not coming a long."

"Why not?"

"Because, they just aren't"

"You know jealousy is a bad thing. It can eat away at you and make you bitter. Do you want to be bitter the rest of your life?"

Emeri was upset. This was the second time she had been called jealous in one afternoon. She was beginning to take offense.

"Are you insinuating that I am bitter?"

"Emeri, you are." He stated plain and clear.

"I'm not bitter; I'm upset with how things turned out."

He gave her a sympathetic look, "Sounds like bitter baby."

She gave a small half smile. She did sound bitter, "Well maybe a little."

"Why are you doing this?"

"Doing what?"

"Allowing me to stay here?"

"Because you're my daughter, if I don't love you and try to take care of you, who will?"

"Me."

"I'm sure you would do a great job. But, I like having you here with me. Who knows, maybe if you were to open up and let us get to know you and vice versa, you may come to love us as well."

Emeri seriously doubted that. Love him and Ma Cyn yes. Naima, no.

"I already love you and Ma Cyn."

"And Naima?" He asked.

"The jury is still out on that one."

"Emeri, come here."

As he put his tools down and whiped his hands on a towel, she walked over to him, he gazed down at her with those kind loving brown eyes and asked, "Do you think me and Cynthia can't love you both?"

"It's not that."

"We can't go back and relive your childhood. I would give anything to have been there to watch you grow up into the beautiful woman that you are today. Anything." His voice trailed off, "But, this crazy obsession you have with Naima has to stop. If you ever stopped being resentful of her long enough to talk to her, you would know she's gone through a lot in her life. She got pregnant at sixteen, was married by eighteen, Kaden was drafted into the NFL by the time she turned twenty-one. He continuously cheated on her; her life was spread across the tabloids, try having almost the entire world knowing your business, and to top that off, her best friend was cheating with Kaden as well. So, don't be so quick to judge, everyone has their own demons they deal with."

While Naima's life was sad, in Emeri's eyes it didn't even begin to compare to hers. Nowhere near, close enough.

Making the decision to tell him about her was a giant leap of faith, but she took it anyway.

"Daddy, I was sexually abused as a child, what about that? Some man abused me from the time I was twelve until I turned eighteen. So, call me judgmental if I refuse to cry rivers for Naima. At the end of the day, she still had it much better than I did and she had the support of two loving parents behind her. My Mama had to work all the time until she was too sick to continue to do so."

"I had no idea about your past." There were tears gleaming in Kenneth's eyes. I'm sorry I couldn't be there to protect you. I never would have allowed that to happen to you."

"I know. But, it's too late for that now. Life is what it is and I am making the most of it my own way."

It saddened Kenneth to see his baby girl tormented like this. Yet she was determined to live her life this way and he could see no change in sight. Emeri was going to be who she was going to be and he was to love her anyway, in spite of herself. Besides, lately he had bitten off more than he could chew. Why he waited till his late fifties to make his life this complicated was beyond him. He was way too old for the mess he was gong through. Shaking his head, he had no one to blame but himself.

Seated at PF Chang's in White Flint Mall waiting for Tyson, Emeri felt her cell vibrate and sighed as she saw who was calling her. Camille had been blowing her phone up nonstop lately. Part of Emeri loved her because she had been there when Emeri really needed someone, it was probably more or less a vendetta she was trying to score with Naima when she first sought Emeri out while she was serving her time. Either way Camille had been a comfort to her and when she was released, the beautiful moments they shared would always be just that. Camille seemed to be having a hard time letting go.

When her cell vibrated a second time, she answered, "Yes, Camille."

"Where the hell do you get off threatening my sister?"

Emeri had not expected that outburst, but it only took her about two seconds to regroup.

"I think you better calm down." She told Camille softly.

"Fuck you Emeri. I'm not Coleen. You're not pulling that shit with me. How could you disrespect our friendship by doing that?"

"Look, your sister was getting above herself. She needed to be brought down a notch or two. Deal with it." Emeri was upset with herself for entertaining this conversation, "Are you done"

"Bitch, you're going to get yours. This is not over!" Camille hung up the phone.

Emeri stared at the disconnected receiver in her hand. That did it Camille had to go. No one threatened her and got away with it. No one. She was a great girl, but she had overstepped her boundaries this time and she would pay, her and her precious sister Coleen.

Smiling as Tyson approached the table, Emeri pushed all thoughts of Camille and Coleen far out of her head to focus her attention on the sexy man joining her.

Leaning down placing a light kiss on her lips, Tyson wondered what was wrong with him. He needed to have his head examined. There was no denying that Emeri was a beautiful woman. The tosseled crinkly black curls, slanted light brown eyes and elongated slim model silhouette would make any man drool. But he was putting his livelihood in jeopardy by seeing her out in the open like this and yet he couldn't stop himself.

"Hey babe. How are you?" he said as he took the vacant seat across from her.

"I'm doing ok."

"That's it? Just ok."

Chestnut eyes gazed up at her. He was so gorgeous. She wondered if this was how Naima felt when she looked at Kaden.

"Yeah, it definitely looks more promising now that you're here."

Tyson smiled, "Is that so?"

"Very much so."

Feeling like now was the perfect time to voice his concerns about their possible lives moving forward he laid all his cards out on the table.

"Emeri, I think I should recommend a new therapist for you." Her face instantly fell.

"What? Why?!"

"Because it's inappropriate for me to counsel and date you at the same time," He gave her an inquiring look, "Can't you see the conflict of interest?"

She could feel the tears threatening to spill.

"But I don't want another therapist. I trust you." Looking at him with pain filled eyes Emeri couldn't comprehend why he would do something like this. "Don't do this to me."

"Babe, why are you acting this way? I'm saying to you that I want to continue dating you, but I would also like to keep my job."

"I understand what you're saying," she trailed off.

"Taking her hands into his; as her therapist Tyson understood what she was dealing with. Emeri suffered from separation anxiety, among other things. Even though he would still be in her life in one aspect, he was exiting from another and that's the part she was having a hard time coping with.

"I'm still going to be around baby, I'm not going anywhere. Trust me, I won't leave you."

Tyson knew that Emeri was fragile, no matter how tough she tried to make herself seem to the rest of the world.

Emeri was skeptical. She was just beginning to trust Tyson and he pulled this stunt. First he would stop the therapy sessions and then he would leave her. She should have known she couldn't trust a man. When had she ever been awarded that luxury? He was like all the rest. Only thinking of himself. What about her? Removing her hands from Tyson's she picked up a napkin to wipe her face. Tears were for the weak and weak she was not.

Tyson felt her withdrawal immediately. He knew she was writing him off and he wasn't going to stand for it.

"Em, don't do this. If you want us to continue our sessions that's fine. I wasn't trying to hurt you."

"I'm not hurt, you're right, you should find someone else for me to have my sessions with."

"Emeri."

Fixating her eyes on his, "Tyson, it's fine," she said with a note of finality. Let's just have dinner.

Tyson knew it wasn't fine, his only concern was how "fine" it really was.

Later that evening…

Having thought long and hard about she and Tyson's situation, Emeri was willing to give him the benefit of the doubt. Now that he wouldn't be counseling her, she was interested to see if he held true to his word, if so, all would be fine and they could run off into the sunset or some shit and be just like Naima and Kaden were. The two of them always seemed so happy with one another. Maybe she and Tyson could have something like that; it would be nice to experience someone loving her that way just once in her lifetime.

"We'll see." She said to herself, as her thoughts switched to more pressing matters like Camille and Coleen, the whoring Hunter sisters, both sleeping with married men, neither giving a shit about it. Emeri wondered what would happen if secrets came to light. It may be time for the sisters to have a little fall. "Yes, that seemed appropriate," she thought as she hummed the nursery rhyme "Humpty Dumpty sat on a wall."

"I cannot believe what you are telling me. What do you mean you are going to fix your marriage with Haven? What the fuck?! This was not part of our deal and you know it.!" Camille was beyond pissed off. Who did Chris think he was?

"Camille, calm down. It's not what you're making it out to be."

"Oh, it better not be, because if I find out you've been playing games this entire time, there will be hell to pay."

"You need to relax and do it now." He said.

Not backing down for a second, Camille was heated, "Don't you talk to me like that. I'll relax when I see fit to relax."

"Hit me back when you calm down." Chris said as he hung up. He was tired of dealing with Haven and Camille. His arrangement with Haven was all business, now that Kadir was here things could go on as originally planned. But in order for that to happen, things with Camille needed to be cooled down for a while. He'd thought she would understand that, but apparently not.

Having made amends with Haven, he had moved back into the house. She seemed willing to forgive him, just as he had 'forgiven' her. They both knew it was only a matter of time before the world they were living in was drastically changed forever.

Chapter 12

S he had been officially cleared to walk unaided by a cane, walker, anything and she could not be happier. God bless physical therapists everywhere. Hers had mentioned to her that she might need her cane sometimes, if she was going to walk for long periods but that for the most part, she was good to go. Naima was elated she had to take her time, but soon she would be running around with Kalani and that made her happy.

She was home in the kitchen trying to get dinner together since Kaden would be home with the kids soon. Ever since their talk in her office, he had been a lot more attentive, now that he was also jobless, she hoped he would find something to occupy his time. Working for Damir had afforded him the opportunity to make some great connections, that coupled with the connections he already had from his football days, should mean he would be able to find work sooner than later.

Kaden was still up to something though. He was being so secretive about everything. Naima had even tried talking to her mom about it, but her mother was on his side this time. "Chile, stop worrying over nothing, Kaden's not up to no good." She'd said. Since when Kaden had an ally in her mother was still a mystery. All Naima knew, was that it better not be another woman. The time in her life of forgiving Kaden of his indiscretions had come and gone. Not that she wasn't guilty of the same thing and by no means were her actions excusable, but Kaden had done enough dirt to last ten men a lifetime. Any foolishness this time and she was going to do what she should have done a long time ago if she had had any sense, get a divorce and move on with her life. She had a teenage daughter to be concerned about this time around and Namiyah would be dating soon. Naima felt it was her job to teach her the correct way for a man and woman to be in a relationship and cheating should not be tolerated.

Jumping a little as the front door banged open interrupting her thoughts, Naima smiled as she heard, "Ma!" screamed into the air, "I'm in here." She said as she braced herself. Kalani was on his way. Running into the kitchen at full speed, he threw himself right into her waiting arms.

"Hey boo bear." She looked down at him, "How was your day?"

"It was great. At recess today my friend TJ fell because he was running too fast and Charles stuck his foot out and TJ went boom, boom. boom." He demonstrated as he fell on the kitchen floor rolling and laughing.

"Kalani, that is not funny," Naima lightly scolded with a giggle, "Was he ok?"

"Ah Mom, he was ok." Looking at his Mom with a side grin, Kalani couldn't help adding, "and it was funny." Still laughing he ran out the kitchen.

Naima had to laugh in spite of herself. Boys will be boys.

She was still smiling when Namiyah came in to give her a hug, "Do you need help fixing dinner?"

"Sure, I would love that. Where's your Dad?"

"He had to run back out. A meeting or something. He said to tell you he would make it back in time for dinner though, so please set a place for him."

"Oh, ok." Naima wondered where it was he had to go. "How have your sessions been going with Coleen," she asked, turning her thoughts back to Namiyah, "Do you want to talk about it?"

She was standing in front of the sink rinsing off the asparagus they were going to have for dinner, "It's going ok. I like Coleen. She's really sweet and she doesn't force me to talk about things I don't want to talk about. She's pretty cool."

"See, so your Mom's not such a bad guy for insisting you go right?"

She laughed as she came over to give her a hug, "No Ma, you're not a bad guy, now a bad girl maybe."

Naima laughed flicking the kitchen towel at her, "Get outta her girl." Namiyah picked up a towel and flicked hers back, "Oh, it's on now." She laughed.

"That's not fair." Naima said in merriment, "You can move faster than I can."

"Excuses, excuses. It's ok to say you're old."

Naima's mouth dropped open in horror, and she fell into a fit of giggles, "Old jokes huh? Ok, I got your old." Grabbing a canister of flour, she filled the scoop cup to the top and tossed it on Namiyah.

Namiyah's shocked face was pure comedy. While she was still off guard, Naima tossed another scoop of flour on her.

Dropping the towel, running over to the sink, Namiyah filled a pitcher of water, Naima shouted, "Don't you dare!" But it fell on deaf ears. Namiyah poured the whole pitcher of water on top of her head. Sliding to the floor in a fit of laughter, "Truce!!!" Naima yelled.

Kalani came to the kitchen doorway, "What are you guys doing in here?"

"Mommy just lost the kitchen war. Go get a camera." Namiyah told him.

"Cool." He said as he took off down the hall to find a camera.

"Dare I ask what happened to the kitchen?"

Naima was already smiling before she responded, "See what happens when you aren't home. You miss all the good stuff." She said as she combed through her freshly washed hair, "Namiyah and I had a kitchen war. I can't remember the last time we had so much fun together."

"Well who lost," he paused, "the kitchen?"

"Ha Ha Kaden. Whatever." She laughed.

"I'm glad you two had fun. I guess that puts me on the clean up committee of one huh?"

"Serves you right for missing dinner," Naima said as she stood up to give him a kiss, "Where you been babe? I missed you."

"I was out taking care of some business."

"Oh, well I left your dinner warming in the oven."

"Thanks baby."

"Can we talk about something that's been on my mind?"

Reaching up to pull his shirt off, Naima couldn't help staring at his bare skin. Her husband was so sexy to her.

"Of course Mocha. We can talk about anything you like."

"I've given this a lot of thought and playing with Namiyah this evening only reinforced it," she took a deep breath before she continued, "How would you feel about adopting? You know I always wanted more children before the incident, just because I can't have any doesn't mean there aren't plenty of kids out there that don't need a loving home."

Kaden thought about that for a moment. It's not that he cared either way about the kids, they could afford it. He was more concerned with Naima's crazy sister Emeri and if they were being smart responsible adults by bringing unsuspecting children into the situation. Their kids were born into it, so that made things a little different.

"Am I to take your silence as a no? You don't have to decide now. I just wanted to put it out on the table as an option."

"I'll think about it." Raising his signature eyebrow, Kaden looked into Naima's eyes, "Would my wife care to join me in the Jacuzzi? I think I may be a teenie bit jealous of you playing with the kids. How about playing with your husband for a little while, or the rest of the night?"

"Mmmm, I thought you would never ask." Naima said, though she had just recently gotten out of the shower, "You know playing with my husband is my favorite hobby of all time." Already removing her robe, "Last one in has to clean up the kitchen AND fix breakfast for the kids in the morning."

Kaden lagged behind as he watched her slowly move her nude body in the direction of the Jacuzzi. This was one race he didn't mind losing, as far as he was concerned, as he continued to watch his beautiful wife, he had already won.

Camille was frustrated beyond reason. Chris had pulled back

from her life, she pretty much kicked Emeri out of her life and now she was lonely. Coleen was off playing mistress and Mommy. Which reminded her; she had company coming over shortly. She needed some damn friends, someone who could help her deal with the Emeri situation. Something had to be done. Emeri would not get away with threatening Coleen. Shit was not going down like that. Coleen wanted her to leave the situation alone, but she knew that wasn't Camille's style. If she wanted it left alone, she never should have mentioned it in the first place. The only question was what to do about it. Hearing the doorbell ring, she was grateful for the interruption, her company had arrived

Arriving across the street, watching Camille's and another silhouette in the dimly lit house, Emeri bid her time wisely. Seeing Coleen's car in the driveway she smiled maybe she could get lucky and have a two for one deal tonight. Having learned her lesson from the Damir and Amber incident, this time she was smart enough to leave her car at home and hike on foot. Her hair was pulled back under a black afro wig, face devoid of make-up with a stocking mask covering it, dressed in all black with running shoes on, she blended in with the trees. Checking to make sure, she had all the necessary materials she was ready to get to work.

The moon was hiding behind clouds tonight giving Emeri enough darkness to move about undetected. Creeping to the back of Camille's house, she took out the key Camille had given her and entered the house through the basement. The room was pitch black, so Emeri had to feel her way, luckily Camille was an avid neat freak and her home stayed clean and in order, which tonight worked to Emeri's benefit. Hearing talking coming from the kitchen, Emeri slowly ascended the basement stairs. Opening the door slowly, praying that the hinges wouldn't creak, she listened. She heard Camille's voice still coming from the direction of the kitchen and nothing else throughout the rest of the house. Quietly closing the basement door behind her, Emeri made her way up the stairs to the bedrooms. Going into each bedroom, she opened the windows to let in oxygen, and left linseed oil soaked cloths in a can beneath each bed. Hanging onto the banister in the hall, she could still hear Camille speaking in the kitchen. Making a swift descent down the stairs, Emeri went around the rest of the house opening windows and leaving whiskey bottles. Concluding in the den, she was thoroughly satisfied with her work. Inaudibly easing her way back into the basement, Emeri was ready for her plan to go into full effect. Leaving one last can by the basement door, she waited until she could see light and smoke coming from it, then she slipped out the house unnoticed.

Flicking through channels in her room, as Chris was feeding Kadir in the nursery, Haven was happy to have some down time. It had been awhile since she'd had a newborn in the house and she vowed to herself that this would be the last one. No more babies were coming out of this body if she could help it. The way things were going with Chris, she didn't think that would be a problem anyway. He hadn't touched her since before the baby was born and that was fine with her.

Finding nothing on TV, she settled on the news. "Let's see who else's life is more fucked up in the world than mine." She said to herself.

Haven watched the usual traffic jams on the hated 495 beltway in Maryland and Virginia. She hated taking the beltway for anything. If she could help it, she always tried to take the back roads, which were much better for a person's sanity.

Leaving the news on, she picked up the phone to dial Naima.

"Hey Girl! What's going on?"

"Wow, why are you so animated?"

"Whoo girl! Just finished loving my man real good," Haven could hear her giggling on the other end of the phone.

"I'm jealous."

"You should be."

"I'm happy for you." Haven really was happy for Naima. She had always wanted someone to look at her the way Kaden did and say the things that Kaden said to Naima. Shaking her head, she didn't foresee it happening in this lifetime.

"Thanks girlie. How are things over there with you and Chris? Is he keeping his hands to himself?

"Yeah, there have been no repeat incidents of abuse." Haven closed her eyes as she spoke; she just realized how tired she was.

"Good. I don't' know what has gotten into Chris. Was he like this in college?"

"Not at all. That Chris was wonderful. I ruined that guy when I sent him to jail. It's my fault he's the way he is now."

Naima didn't say anything. Opening her eyes in the wake of silence, Haven was shocked to see Naima's Dad's picture on the screen, she sat up suddenly.

"Nai, do you have you TV on?"

"No, why? What's wrong?" Naima asked hearing the urgency in Haven's voice.

"Turn to the news quick, your Dad's picture is on there."

"Are you serious? What are they saying? Shoot, I can't find the remote."

"Wait a minute. They're saying something about a fire." Reaching for her remote, she turned the TV up to hear the news reporter.

"Behind me, a house caught fire on the eighteenth block of Lee Drive earlier this evening. The cause of the fire has yet to be determined, we do have news that two individuals were inside the house. We have confirmation that both victims have been pronounced dead. We here at Fox 5 send our condolences to the families of Camille Hunter and Kenneth Vaughn.

"Oh my God. This can't be true, it can't." A broken up Naima said over the phone.

"I don't believe it either. I'm so sorry. Do you need me to come over?"

"No, oh my God," She said again. "I have to check on my Mom." Haven could hear her sobbing on the other end of the line, "I don't know what to do."

"Ok, I'm on my way. I'll meet you at your Mom's."

Haven hung up the phone, "Chris!" she yelled as she got up to go to the closet to put on some sweats. Having downed the sweats and still seeing no sign of Chris, she began walking toward the nursery where he had been feeding Kadir. Not finding him in there, she saw a dim light coming from his study. She pushed the door open slowly, "Chris," she said softly. She found him holding a sleeping Kadir in his arms with tears coming down his face. The Channel 7 news was on and they were recapping the fire incident.

Haven watched as her husband cried for his mistress with their child in his arms and shut the door quietly to not disturb her sleeping baby. Her eyes mirrored his pain, as much as she would have loved to do or say something, she couldn't, she had to get to Naima's Mother's house. Her friend was more important right now, than anything, she and Chris were dealing with. Leaving a note saying where she would be she left.

Arriving at the Vaughn house, you would have thought it was the Fourth of July. The whole house was lit up it seemed like. Testing the front door to see if it was unlocked, which it was, Haven walked in. Following the sound of the voices, Haven found everyone congregated in the family room.

She thought that Mrs. Cynthia would be the one needing the most consoling, but Emeri was sitting in the middle of the floor crying her eyes out damn near hyperventilating and Mrs. Cynthia was consoling her. Kaden was doing his best to calm a weeping Naima and Namiyah and Kalani were sitting there not saying a word.

Haven was at a loss for what to do. She went over to the kids to see how they were holding up. Kneeling down on the floor in front of them, she touched Namiyah and Kalani on their knees.

"Hey guys, how are you feeling?" Kalani didn't seem connected to what was going on, but Namiyah was trying hard to hold back her tears. Reaching up Haven pulled her into a hug. Haven smoothed Namiyah's long hair back, "It's ok honey. You can let it out. Your God Mommy is here."

Namiyah broke at that moment. She lost the fight to be strong willed and allowed the tears to fall. She couldn't believe that her Granddaddy was gone. She had a crazy Aunt, her Granddad was pronounced dead, what planet was she on? Why was he at that women's house anyway? Hugging her Godmother back as hard as she could, she was fed up with this crazy life.

"I didn't even know Daddy knew Camille." Naima said to no one in particular as she wiped the tears from her eyes. She watched her mother comfort a distressed Emeri, which angered her. Her mother was the one that just lost her husband and though she seemed to be fairing the best out of all of them, she should be the one being comforted.

"Momma, you should sit down," Naima said, "Are you doing ok?"

"Chile, you know I can't sit and rest with all these folks in my house. I'll be back, I made hot cider for everyone."

Naima followed her Mom to the kitchen, "Momma stop, I'll take the tray," Naima said as her Mother sat the last cup of piping hot cider on top of it. Grabbing a hold of her arm forcing her Mother to look at her, she tried again.

"Momma, you don't have to be so tough all the time. This is Daddy, it's ok to cry." But Naima knew her mother, as long as the sky stayed up above and the ground down below, Cynthia Vaughn would not shed a tear for the world to see.

"Baby, you and Emeri are crying enough for me. I'll be fine. Now shoo, take that tray for me and I'll be out in a minute."

Naima picked up the tray as she was told and rejoined everyone in the living room. Cynthia picked up a rag to wipe off the counter and noticed Kenneth's favorite whiskey glass sitting there. Lord how that man loved his whiskey, she thought with a half smile. Picking it up slowly, the tears slowly ran down her cheeks. Her husband would never drink out of his favorite glass again. The reality of that came down on her like a ton of bricks. Placing the glass in the sink, she retrieved her rag and cried as she finished cleaning the kitchen.

Across town

Coleen had just finished putting Justin down for the night when her cell phone rang. Shocked to see her Mother's name appear on the screen she answered, "Hey Mom."

"Coleen baby, you're ok."

Huh? She thought, "Yeah, I'm ok. Why wouldn't I be?"

"I was afraid you might have been over Camille's this evening."

"Mother, you're not making any sense, why would you be afraid I was over Camille's? Why would it matter where I was?"

"Oh sweetie, it's all over the news."

"What? What's all over the news?" Coleen was baffled, as she looked for her remote so she could cut the TV on and see what had her Mother in such an uproar.

Finally locating her remote, which she had put on top of the TV to keep out of Justin's reach, Coleen cut on the TV turning to the news.

"Mom, what's on the news?"

"Camille baby. Her house burned down tonight."

Coleen dropped the phone as Camille and Kenneth's faces came onto the screen. She saw the fire fighters in the background still attempting to dowse the flames. She began to shake her head in disbelief. This could not be happening to her family. Hearing her name being called, Coleen returned the phone from where it had landed.

"I'm here."

"You alright?" Coleen's whole body shook. No she was not alright.

"Coleen. Coleen" Her mother was frantically calling her name.

"Mom, I'm here."

"Maybe you and Justin should come here for a little while."

"Tomorrow Mom, I promise. I have to go." Practically hanging up on her mother Coleen fought to get her thoughts and emotions in check, what was she going to do with her life now?

Chapter 13

Emeri had fucked up royally. Sitting in her room after Kenneth's funeral waiting for all the visitors to pay their respects to the family, she felt like shit. When she'd set Camille's house on fire, she had no idea that the visitor that was there was her Father. Feeling the moisture on her cheek, she brushed the unwelcomed tears away. She was now an orphan in the world and there was no one to blame but herself. This was a huge mistake, big, colossal. She had never intended for Kenneth to get hurt.

Hearing a soft knock on the door, she turned and wiped the remaining tears away, "Come in," she said.

Tyson strolled in joining her on the bed. It was obvious from her tear-streaked face that she wasn't feeling the greatest.

"Do you want to talk?" He offered.

"No."

"Do you mind if I sit here with you?"

"No."

"Are you going to say anything other than no?"

"Tyson, I'm not ready to talk. When I am, I will let you

know. In the meantime can you just lay here with me not asking questions?"

"You got it pretty lady. I'm hear when you're ready."

"I know you are and I'm thankful for that."

Namiyah was the one to answer the door for Coleen when she arrived at the Vaughn house with her cute son from the photos in her office. She was glad to see Coleen, she had seen her at her Granddad's funeral earlier but before that she hadn't seen her since before her sister died. Coleen had cancelled all of their therapy sessions until further notice.

"Hi Coleen."

"Hello Namiyah," Coleen said as she clenched her son's hand tightly, "is it alright if we come in?"

"Sure," Namiyah said as she moved aside to let the two of them enter. Coleen looked a mess. Her face was red and puffy, eyes almost swollen shut as if she had been hit by a two by four. Her son on the other hand looked so handsome in his little black suit clutching his ninja toy. "Mostly everyone is in the basement. If you're looking for Gram, she's in the kitchen with my Mom."

"I want to see your Gram. Thanks sweetie, I'll find the way."

Coleen had only been there once before for the counseling session with Emeri, but she was sure she could figure it out. Locating the kitchen relatively easy, she saw most of the family in there.

Cynthia was the first to notice Coleen hovering in the doorway. She walked over to receive her with a hug.

"What a nice surprise. I saw you at the church, but didn't get a chance to say hello."

Coleen returned the hug she offered. "I wanted to speak as well, but decided to just stop by the house to see you." Looking at Cynthia, "Is there somewhere private we can talk?"

"Yeah, we can go into the sunroom. It should be empty." Noticing the little boy by Coleen's side, Cynthia offered to have him join the other children.

"No," Coleen quickly stated, "I prefer for him to stay with me."

As she followed Cynthia down the hall, Coleen couldn't help but take notice of the many photos that lined the halls. On the outside, the Vaughn's seemed like your typical American family, it wasn't until a person delved deeper did they find out how corrupt and tormented their family really was.

Sitting in one of the chairs in the room, Cynthia pointed to another for Coleen to have a seat.

"What's on your mind Dear?"

Coleen had no idea how to begin. All of her psychological training went out the window. She had no idea how to bring up the topic she needed to discuss with Cynthia. Figuring the direct approach was always best, especially with a no nonsense type of woman such as Cynthia, Coleen forged ahead.

"I was wondering when the meeting for Kenneth's will reading will be taking place, or if his lawyer has contacted you as of yet because I haven't received notification."

Cynthia was confused by this conversation. Why did Coleen care about Kenneth's will?

"As a matter of fact, our lawyer has contacted me, but I don't see why that would concern you."

"It concerns me because I need to make sure Justin is taken care of."

"Who is Justin?"

Coleen nodded her head in her son's direction. "That is Kenneth's son."

"Momma! Momma! Wake up" Cynthia opened her eyes slowly to Naima frantically calling her name. Trying to sit up, Cynthia had no idea how she had come to be lying on the floor.

"What in the world happened?"

"You passed out Mommy. And it's no wonder, you're probably under too much stress. If Coleen hadn't been in here to break your fall, who knows what could have happened. You need to rest."

Hearing Coleen's name jarred Cynthia to full awareness. She saw her standing in the corner and everything she told her came flooding back to the surface.

"You need to leave my home. You are not welcome here." Coleen's face turned crimson.

Naima stood back shocked; her Mom never spoke to anyone that way. What was going on?

"Momma, Coleen tried to help you. She didn't do anything, Why are you being so rude to her?"

"Naima, stay out of this." Cynthia reprimanded lightly, "You don't know what you're talking about." Addressing Coleen again, Cynthia said, "I asked you to leave."

Snatching up Justin's hand, Coleen was mortified. Trying to do exactly as Cynthia had suggested, she ran smack into Emeri who materialized in the doorway. Standing eye-to-eye Emeri smirked at her. Not knowing what got into her, Coleen smacked her with all the strength she could muster, knocking the smirk clean off Emeri's face.

Emeri grabbed her face in shock, and then tackled Coleen to

the ground. "You whoring bitch!"

Letting Justin's hand go as Emeri took her down, so he wouldn't get hurt, Coleen braced for the fall.

"I know you had something to do with their death's you psycho bitch," she spat out as they wrestled on the floor, "And when I prove it, the state is going to fry your ass."

Naima and the family watched in horror as Emeri continuously pounded her fist into Coleen's face. Kaden was the only one brave enough to pick a swinging, kicking, biting Emeri off Coleen. Naima looked around for Tyson and he was nowhere in sight; She could not believe what was going on; everyone was behaving like raving lunatics and for what?

The family watched as Kaden carried Emeri out of the room.

"Namiyah, take Coleen's son downstairs so he doesn't have to witness anymore of this." Naima said.

"No, don't any of you touch my son!" A swollen beat down Coleen yelled from the floor.

Speaking slowly and patiently, Naima tried to reason with her, Emeri had messed up her face pretty bad. Her lips were busted, her left eye was already turning blue and black, teeth marks were visible on her cheeks and blood was oozing out of a cut above her right eye.

"Coleen, let me help you get cleaned up. No one here is going to hurt your son."

Pulling herself off the floor slowly, Coleen was not having it. She didn't want anything from this family except to make sure Justin was taken care of.

"That won't be necessary, we're leaving. Turning to Cynthia she said, "My lawyer will be in touch." Marching across the room grabbing Justin's hand she left, practically dragging him behind her.

Naima was at a loss for words. Her Mother was still sitting on the floor from having passed out, Kaden was somewhere in the house trying to calm a crazed Emeri and the house was still packed with friends paying their respects.

"Momma, what in the world is going on? I've never seen you be so rude in my life." Naima bent down to help her mother to her feet as she waited for a response.

"I need to lay down Chile. Today has been a trying day." She turned before exiting the room, "Naima can you thank everyone for coming, but to please excuse my absence , I need to rest."

"Of course Momma, anything."

"Thanks baby."

Naima was genuinely concerned. This behavior was completely out of character for her Mother. Looking over at Haven who was seated in the corner, she watched her shrug her shoulders.

"I have no idea what just happened either."

"Ok, good." Naima said sitting down next to her, "I thought I was the only one losing my mind for a second."

"No girl, you are not. What do you think Coleen meant when she said she knew Emeri was responsible?" Haven's eyes widened in horror, "You don't think Emeri set Camille's house on fire do you?"

"I wondered about that myself, but it doesn't make sense, why would she burn down Camille's house, especially with our Dad there? It doesn't add up."

"Why was your Dad there?"

"You know, that's the same question I've been asking myself

since I found out about the fire. Nothing about this situation is making any sense."

"That's for damn sure. This place and these crazy sequences of events are pure madness."

"Speaking of madness, how is Chris holding up?"

Rolling her eyes at the ceiling, Haven hated to even discuss her home issues and how Chris was moping in corners and shit crying over Camille.

"Ugh, he's crying all over the place looking crazy. I didn't sign up for this dumb shit."

All Naima could do was listen, rather than say anything, because in all actuality Haven did sign up for this and she continued to stay signed on even after she knew what the deal was with Chris and Camille. Deciding silence on the topic was the best course of action, Naima wisely changed the subject.

"Maybe I should check on Emeri."

"Why? She can handle her own. She doesn't like you anyway, why waste your breath?"

"Because she's still my sister and she lost her Dad too. Now she has no one."

"Mmugh, suit yourself." Haven rose to her feet, "I think I'm going to go. Kaven and Kadir both need to be feed and put to bed." She gave Naima a hug and a kiss on the cheek. "If you need me you know you can call anytime."

Naima returned her hug, "I know. Thanks for coming by the house today. I appreciate it."

"Girl stop, don't even mention it." Haven turned yelling down the hall, "Kaven, let's go! I'm in the car." She turned back to face Naima, "Aight girl, I'm out." She said making her way to the front door, "Remember, call me if you need anything."

Naima smiled, "I will, I promise."

Kaven came running past her at full speed trying to get out the door, "Ah, excuse me," Naima said playfully putting her hands on her hips and pouting, "Are you just going to run out the door and not hug your God Mommy goodbye? Shame on you. You're not too big for hugs already are you?"

Immediately reversing, he came back and gave her a hug. "I'm never too old for hugs from you." He told her, "but you know my Mom hates to wait. I don't want to get left."

Laughing at him, Naima had to agree. When Haven was ready to go, she was ready to go and if you didn't want to get left your best bet was to be at the car standing there waiting on her.

Boy, you ain't never lied. Go ahead and run out there before your Momma leaves you."

"Ok, love you God Mommy."

"Love you too." Naima responded to him as he ran out to the waiting car.

People were finally starting to leave and Naima had never in her life been so happy to see people go. She knew they meant well, but the family had business to tend to that couldn't be done in a house full of people.

At long last, around ten that night, she waved the last well wisher off. Kaden joined her in the foyer as she was closing the door. Noticing the exhausted look on her face, she still was the most beautiful woman in the world to him.

"How you holding up Mocha?"

Before she could acknowledge him, Naima had to kick off her shoes and massage each foot. Effortlessly lifting her off the floor into his arms, Kaden kissed her on the forehead while leading her to the couch. Sitting her at on end, he moved to the opposite end so he could massage her feet for her, he looked at her expectantly, "You didn't answer my question."

Thoroughly enjoying her foot massage Naima let out a tired sigh, "I'm sorry baby, what did you ask me?"

"I asked you how you were holding up."

"I'm doing. How is Emeri? I meant to check on her and got distracted."

"She was pretty riled up when I took her out of here earlier. I'm not sure how she's doing now. I left when Tyson came in."

"Speaking of him, where was he when she was in here trying to practically kill Coleen?"

Kaden shrugged, "Don't know, but he reappeared to check on her, so I rolled."

Naima rubbed her aching temple. "Baby thanks for the massage. I needed it." Unenthusiastically removing her foot from his miracle working fingers, "I have to check on Momma and see how she's doing. She just wasn't herself today. I'm worried about her."

Kaden was not happy to have his massage session with her cut short. "Mocha, she just lost her husband, of course she's not herself."

"True, but Daddy passed away almost a week ago and she didn't behave like she did today. She was straight up rude to Coleen. Momma never behaves so poorly."

"She probably found out that Coleen and our Dad were having an affair and that little boy of Coleen's is actually our brother."

Kaden and Naima's heads turned in unison toward the doorway. Neither had heard Emeri approach. Naima was the first to regain her composure, "What," she whispered, "that can't be true. Daddy would never."

"It is true dear sister and don't say Daddy could never, because if that were the case I wouldn't be standing her now."

"Isn't that the truth?" Naima said to herself.

"Oh no. Coleen must have come here to tell Momma that. No wonder she was being so rude to her." Dropping her head into her hands, Naima felt a migraine coming on; she was beyond disappointed in her Dad, "Poor Momma."

Chapter 14

Running down the dark alleyway, frantically trying to make sure she didn't trip and crack her face, Haven was beyond terrified. All she knew was that somehow, some way, he was going to make it his business to kill her. She could see it in his eyes, when he first began chasing her, this time there would be no moment of return.

Taking a quick breath as she awakened from her nightmare, Haven rolled over to Chris staring her in the face, which was just as unsettling as her dream had been. Body still trembling from the range of emotions that it believed itself to have gone through; Haven couldn't shake the uneasy feeling that something about their whole situation wasn't right. As afraid as she was for her life, there iwas no way to get away from it. Chris was like a time bomb waiting to ignite. He wasn't doing anything out of the ordinary per se. It was just that there seemed to be a dark side within him. Some place inside him that not even God himself could reach. If nothing else, she did accredit him with getting her back into church. She needed God on her side more than anything, so she could survive her life.

She was becoming uncomfortable in her own skin. Ever since Camille's death, Chris was damn near impossible to deal with. If he wasn't moping around, then he was watching Haven. And the way he watched her made her skin crawl. The house was mostly quiet now with occasional interruptions of Kadir crying and Kaven's noisy banter. There were no words between her and Chris however. At first Haven was perfectly fine with the quiet, but now his silence was deadly. It was like walking on eggshells in this place.

Kadir's sudden cry over the baby monitor offered Haven the perfect excuse to get out of bed away from Chris. Jumping up immediately, she went to the aid of their baby.

Coleen was irate with what her lawyer told her. Kenneth had neglected to change his will once Justin was born. He had changed it when he found out about Emeri, but no dice when it came to Justin. She was tempted to contest it but her lawyer told her unless they could find a loophole in the document somewhere, there was nothing that could be done. Don't get her wrong, it's not that she couldn't take care of Justin on her own, because she could more than afford to. She just wanted him to be able to have some mementos from his father's life and the way Cynthia had reacted, Coleen was more than sure she would not be parting with anything that belonged to Kenneth anytime soon and there was no one on the inside to fight on her behalf. She knew Emeri wouldn't, that crazy hoe. If she wanted any help, Coleen knew Naima was probably her best bet, so she would focus her energy on her.

Switching her thoughts over to more pressing matters,

Coleen was on a mission to prove that Emeri was involved in Camille and Kenneth's murder, but she needed help. Picking up her phone she called the one person who she was more than sure would be as broken up about Camille's death as she was.

"Yes." A flat unemotional voice answered.

"Hi Chris, its Coleen."

"Hey." He replied with the same amount of enthusiasm as he had when he answered the phone.

"You sound the way I feel, so how about us doing something about it?"

"Do something about what?" Coleen ignored his question.

"Why don't you come over? I think Emeri had something to do with Camille's death and I figure between the two of us, we should be able to figure out a way to prove it."

What Coleen was saying instantly peeked Chris' interest. "Do you really think she had something to do with it? That doesn't make sense, why would she be against Camille?"

"When has Emeri ever made any sense?" Coleen asked Chris, he must have forgotten who they were referring to, "If you come over, we can talk about it. I don't really want to say too much over the phone. Emeri is smart, who knows if she has the lines tapped and what not."

"Aight, I'm on my way."

"Ok, see you when you get here."

Coleen practically ran to answer the door when Chris arrived. She had been impatiently pacing the floor for the last hour anticipating his arrival.

"Goodness, I see you finally made it."

Chris gazed at her with indifference in his eyes. As far as he was concerned, he was here like she wanted, who gave a shit how long it took him to get there.

"I'm here right? So tell me the deal." He said as he walked past her into the living room.

Coleen closed the door and followed him to the living room. Chris sat on the sofa and looked at her expectantly.

"I know this will probably devastate you, but Camille and Emeri were more than friends."

Chris frowned his face up. "What is that supposed to mean?"

"Well, it means they were more like kissing friends."

He jumped up off the sofa when she said that. "You're lying!"

Coleen gave him a pointed look, "Chris, don't you think I know what was going on with my own sister?"

"Camille would never do that to me, she loved me."

Coleen nodded her head in affirmation, "Yes, she did love you, but you are married, what was she supposed to do when you were home with your wife and children?"

"She was supposed to wait for me. We had a deal and set plans on a life together."

Coleen looked at him in disbelief not understanding Camille's attraction to him or Emeri, both were extremely selfish.

"You're talking craziness, but either way, you're losing focus on the issue at hand." Coleen proceeded to elaborate, "I made a mistake and told Camille that Emeri had threatened me and that's why I was no longer counseling her. I think she may have tried to confront Emeri and Emeri retaliated by setting her house on fire to get her out of the way. I just have to find a way to prove it."

Chris was astonished. This was a lot more information than

he had anticipated taking in this afternoon. He looked over at Coleen, "So what do you propose we do about this situation? The police are already investigating; we can't interfere with a crime scene or case."

Coleen's eyes sparkled as her speaking became animated, "Well, I have a little background information on Ms. Emeri," Leaning into Chris as if about to tell a grand secret she continued, "Turns out her issues run deep. Camille told me Emeri confided in her once and said that she was molested as a child."

Chris didn't think it was possible for him to be any more shocked than he already was. He stood corrected. His mind flashed back to his own demented childhood. He had never told anyone about the sexual abuse his father had inflicted on him as a child. When his mother found out she immediately kicked his Dad out and divorced him and his Dad had moved to New York somewhere. Chris remembered vowing to hunt his father down when he was able to do so, but he'd never gotten the opportunity. His father had been found murdered in an alley his throat slit. As far as Chris was concerned, that death had been too good for his father. Chris wished he would have suffered more. The only thing he hated more than that was he had his Dad's name. Chris Thomas Jr. All the kids around the neighborhood used to call his Dad Mr.CT and they called him little CT.

That may be the reason Chris could never forgive Haven. Of all the things she could have sent him to jail for, she had claimed rape. Just the thought of it disgusted him. After the childhood he'd lived he would never rape anyone. The false accusation and serving time for a crime he didn't commit was too much for him. He would never forgive her.

Shaking his head trying to clear his mind of his hated

memories, he turned his attention back to Coleen.

"What does that have to do with her causing a fire?" He asked her.

"It shows a pattern of her mental instability."

Chris wondered what school Coleen received her PhD from, because she sounded dumb.

"Coleen, everyone already knows Emeri is mentally unstable. She plead guilty by way of insanity in a murder trial. Doesn't take a genius to see the girl has issues.

Coleen thought about that for a moment. Chris had a point. Emeri already had a pattern of being psycho. Biting down on her lip, she was at a loss of what to say.

Feeling like their conversation was concluded; Chris stood to make an exit. Kissing Coleen on the forehead, he said, "I know you want to blame Emeri, but without proof or motive you have nothing to go on. Let the authorities do their job. If she's guilty they will handle it and this time I'm sure they won't let her loony ass out."

Tears slid down Coleen's face. "I miss my sister, my son doesn't have a father. I know Emeri did this." Wiping the tears with her hand, "I know she did," she whispered again.

Pulling her into a hug Chris held her as he released his own tears for their loss.

Chris couldn't believe what Coleen had told him earlier that day about Camille and Emeri. He never would have guessed anything was up with the two of them, he just thought they were friends. The fact that Coleen also suspected Emeri of being connected to the fire that took Camille's life was crazy, but believable, because who knew what Emeri was capable of.

Coleen knew Chris had a point. Without any real proof, she

couldn't wage a full out war with Emeri. She had a child to look after and knowing what Emeri was capable of, she needed to relax. She was still concerned about the fight they'd had on the day of Kenneth's funeral. She had no idea what came over her that day. But back to back funerals for Camille and Kenneth must have had her on edge and Emeri's smug face was too much for her that day. That whole scene was completely out of character for her, completely out of character.

Naima had just said goodnight to Kalani and was closing his bedroom door when Kaden let her know she had a phone call. Hoping it wasn't Haven with more Chris drama, she braced herself, answering the phone cautiously.

"Hello."

"Hello Naima." The person responded back. Naima waited patiently for them to continue since she was not readily able to identify the voice on the other end of the phone.

"It's Coleen." Naima groaned inwardly. She did not feel like any drama tonight. She just wanted to go to bed with her husband and that's it. Was that to much to ask?"

"Hi Coleen. What can I do for you?" Naima asked rather coldly. Women like Coleen offended her sensibilities. They were the women that she had been fighting to keep out of Kaden's life for as long as she could remember. These women set the whole women's movement back by centuries with their foolish behavior and not finding fault in sexing and loving married men that would never be completely theirs, ruining lives with their unbelievable selfishness.

Coleen knew she was treading on thin ice with Naima, but she had to try.

"Naima, I know I'm probably the last person on earth you want to speak with, but I'm just asking that you hear me out."

Giving Kaden the evil eye for handing her the phone to begin with, Naima went into their room and sat on the bed so she could give Coleen her complete attention.

"I'm listening."

"I know, you're probably as upset as your mother about this whole ordeal. I'm asking if we could put all differences aside and focus on Justin. He is the innocent here and I want to do right by him."

Naima almost laughed out loud. How could one do all the wrong things and then turn around and try to make all those wrongs seem right?

"I do agree that Justin is the innocent in this crazy situation," Naima began slowly, "but, I'm confused as to what you want me to do."

Clearing her throat Coleen responded. "I was hoping you could talk to your mother about a possible inheritance for Justin. I want him to have something of his father's when he gets older."

Naima shut her eyes in exasperation. "Coleen, I cannot promise you anything. My mother will do what she wants to do. But, what I can say is she's always fair, right now she's angry and hurt. She needs time to heal. I'm sure she'll contact you when she's ready."

"But that's no guarantee."

"Nothing in life is a guarantee. We just take the cards we're dealt and play them to the best of our ability, rolling with the punches. You're a therapist, you should know this." Naima could not believe she had let this woman counsel her child.

"It's a little different when you have to apply it to your own life."

"I'm sure it is. Was there anything else that I could help you with?"

"Well," Coleen proceeded with caution, "I was wondering if you would be willing to spend time with Justin? You are his older sister; I would love for him to get to know you."

Naima shook her head, rubbing her hand over her face. She was tired of this crazy rollercoaster ride of a life. Why was life never simple and so complicated?

"Coleen, you never sought out our interaction before, why do you want to now? He's been my brother since he was born."

"I know, but his father was around. Now he doesn't have that. I want him to know all of you and thus be able to understand his Dad when he's older."

Naima finally did laugh then. "I had thirty-two years with my Dad and don't understand what was going on with him. I doubt Justin will be able to since he'll never know him."

"Please Naima." Coleen hated to sound like she was begging but what choice did she really have?

Naima was softening. How could she not? She had a three-year-old brother that was too cute not to spoil.

"Ok Coleen, you can bring Justin by sometime. I won't mind. But as far as my mother is concerned, that whole situation is between the two of you. I have nothing to do with it.

"Ok, fair enough. Thank you so much for agreeing to be a part of Justin's life."

"Don't mention it again. He's family and we Vaughn's are big on family. Goodnight."

"Night."

Coleen hung up happy with the call. Not exactly, everything

she had hoped for, but at least it was a start.

Chapter 15

"I'm the one that set Camille's house on fire." Tyson remained quiet. Emeri looked over at him, "Did you hear what I said?" I did it, but I had no idea my Dad was in there. He was driving Coleen's car that day. I thought she was inside." Covering her face with her hands, for the first time in her life, Emeri was sorry about something that she had done.

"I know," Tyson finally said softly. Emeri jerked her head up.

"What do you mean you know? How could you?"

"Rising from his chair Tyson knelt down in front of her, "I found the linseed oil, cans cloths and a 'How to Guide' when I was in your room the day of the funeral. I disposed of the items for you." Brushing her hair off her forehead, "I don't want to see anything bad happen to you."

It all came back to Emeri now. No wonder he wasn't there when she and Coleen had gotten into it. He was removing incriminating evidence to save her; she didn't know what to say, she was speechless. No man had ever gone out of his way to help her before. This proved Tyson's loyalty to her and to think she had thought about getting rid of him.

Grabbing his face with both hands, she brought hers to his level and searched his eyes, "Why would you do that and risk everything? Your job, your freedom," she paused for a moment, "everything?"

"Because I feel like I can help you. You just need an opportunity to show the world, that you can change. I believe in you."

Once again, Emeri could feel the tears welling up. Good men did exist in the world; men like Tyson proved that and she was glad he was on her side.

Namiyah stood outside Emeri's bedroom door horrified by what she had just heard. Gram had sent her, of all people, to get Emeri for dinner and she'd heard Emeri and Tyson deep in conversation. Now things were beginning to make sense. No wonder she was crying so hysterically and acting a fool when she found out about Grand Dad's death. She was the one responsible for his death and was clearly devastated.

Waiting a full minute before knocking on the door, she heard the animated talking turn into muffled whispers.

"Come in." Emeri called out.

Opening the door slowly, Namiyah poked her head in looking Emeri up and down. "Gram said dinner is ready." She informed her with plenty of attitude then shut the door immediately behind her.

Emeri glanced over at Tyson, "You don't think she heard what we were discussing do you?"

"I don't think so. If she had, don't you think she would have said something?"

"I don't think she would have. That girl is sneaky and something tells me she heard exactly what we were talking about."

"Well," he began, "What are you going to do about it?"

"Hmmn, I don't know yet. I'm going to have to find a way to test her to see what she knows."

"Em, try not to do anything crazy. She's just a kid." He pleaded with her softly.

"She's a kid with an adult mentality. There is nothing kid-like about Namiyah, except her age."

"Ok then, what do you want to do?"

"Go to dinner," purposely misinterpreting his question, "The family is waiting." She said as she opened the bedroom door for her and Tyson to head down to the dinning room.

Cynthia was hoping that just this one day; they could have a nice normal dinner. She never knew what would happen when Namiyah and Emeri shared the same space and air. They didn't think she picked up on the under currents between them, but Cynthia was no fool. She never missed a beat.

Namiyah was already acting oddly. She had a taste more attitude than Cynthia liked, which is why she kept a tight reign on this one. Namiyah was nothing like her mother. Naima had been the sweetest child growing up, a tad naïve, but very sweet.

Looking over at Namiyah; the child sure did look sweet as pie, with her pretty self, but her temperament left something to be desired. Cynthia was trying to comprehend how all of their lives ended up so out of wack. She had always been a God-fearing Christian woman and still was, but when trials came, boy did they come. She knew she had to do the right thing by Coleen and split Kenneth's inheritance so that she would be able to take care of her son, Justin. However, Lord forgive her, she wanted Coleen to suffer just as she had. She had accepted Emeri whole-heartedly and look what mess that had gotten her family into. Now she was supposed to accept a three-year-old little boy. What was wrong with Kenneth? She wished he were here so she could confront him face to face. These were supposed to be her Golden Years; she should be enjoying them, not dealing with her deceased husband's mistress and child, his deranged daughter Emeri, a grand daughter that she was sure was standing on the edge of a cliff ready to jump or push someone off sooner rather than later. Cynthia had never been so angry in her life. "The Lord will never give you more than you can bear." She repeated over and over in her head.

When Emeri and Tyson walked into the dining room, Ma Cyn, Namiyah and Kalani were seated and waiting on them.

"Nice of you two to finally join us Chile, we were about to begin without you."

"Now Ma Cyn, you know I would not miss your cooking for the world. Tyson and I were finishing up a discussion is all."

"Well ya'll sit on down here so we can eat."

Kalani said grace, which was the norm and they all dug in.

Feeling watched Emeri looked up to see Namiyah staring directly at her. Placing her fork on the table, she glared back at her. The tension in the air was undeniable. Cynthia felt it immediately as she glanced first at Emeri and then Namiyah.

Namiyah knew. Emeri could feel it in her bones. The way the girl kept staring at her as if silently daring Emeri to do or say anything that would give her a reason to blurt out what she knew. Emeri remained silent, she wasn't a fool. This wasn't the time or place to address Namiyah. There was no way she wanted

Ma Cyn knowing what she had done, no way at all and as far as Namiyah was concerned, she would get what was coming to her.

Damir was slipping further and further into his depressive slump. Naima never returned his phone calls. He knew Kaden had probably told her what went down in the office that day. In an attempt to save face he had gone to his attorney to see if charges could be brought up against him, but since Damir was the first to attempt assault he was at fault. His attorney had told him he was lucky Kaden didn't sue him, so he should let the situation ride. Now at his job he was considered a joke. Everyone who was present in the office on the day of his and Kaden's fight took to talking behind his back and smirking at him and for those that hadn't been there, they were filled in by their gossiping ass co-workers. He was officially a laughing stock.

Sinking deeper and deeper, he gazed into his glass of Hennessey and coke. Pulling out a pen and writing pad he made a list of things that needed to be done for Alanna. He smiled then; thinking of her always lightened his spirits. Even now, she was upstairs sleeping peacefully. He'd been blessed with an angel for a child. Once upon a time he'd imagined that he and Naima would have been able to raise a family together, but he had underestimated the magnitude of how deep Kaden and Naima's love went for one another. They were that once in a lifetime couple that had that rare true love, the love that some people search their entire lives for. No matter what happened in life, those two would emerge out of it together victorious.

Placing the writing pad and pen on his desk, Damir was happy with the decision he was making, never had anything been so clear to him in his life. Retreating up the steps, he stopped by Alanna's room to check on his baby girl. It still amazed him how much she looked like her mother, Amber. If Amber had lived to see her, she would have wanted her. There's no way you couldn't want Alanna, she was perfect. He leaned down and kissed her on the forehead then walked to his room down the hall and closed the door. Entering his personal bathroom, he stared at himself in the mirror, "Yeah, I'm making the right decision," he said to himself as he closed the bathroom door and welcomed the heavenly sight of his sister Alanna.

"You have been granted custody of Alanna Collins. Damir has selected you to be her legal guardian. Providing that you choose to accept this role you will have to fill out the necessary paperwork and she belongs to you. She is currently staying with Mr. Collin's mother until this is all sorted out."

Naima was in a state of shock at what the caseworker was telling her. What would possess Damir to commit suicide? More importantly, select her as the legal guardian for his child. She had only met his daughter Alanna once. Naima's heart ached for her, that poor baby, no Mommy and no Daddy. This whole situation pulled at her heartstrings.

"This was also left for you. It's a letter from Damir to you. I'll step out for a moment for you to read." The caseworker left the room.

Naima looked over at Kaden and shrugged as she slowly opened the letter,

Naima,

I know you are probably surprised by the current events

taken place before you. You wouldn't return my calls, so I guess I finally have your undivided attention now. After a lot of thinking, you and Kaden deserve each other. I've never seen two people love the way you two do. I've wanted that my whole life and couldn't seem to find it. I didn't even know what true love was until Alanna was born. I have never loved anyone the way I love her. That being said I think she deserves to grow up in an environment where she can see and experience first hand what it is like to witness true love everyday. Once upon a time, I had hoped you and I could make a go at it...but as I stated you and Kaden were made for each other. No one can deny the way love radiates off of you two.

I'm entrusting Alanna to you. You're a great mother and I know you will love her like your own and give her the motherly touch that I'm sure she wants and needs. I would have given her to my parents, but they really don't have the time or agility for an active five year old running around.

I loved you, from the day I met you till now, I still love you. Take care of my baby.
Love,
Damir

Tears welled up in Naima's eyes. Kaden could already see it in Naima's face. She was a goner. She had recently broached the subject of wanting to adopt and through a twist of fate she was being offered a child. He knew there was only a matter of time before there were three children in his home as opposed to two.

He wasn't the least bit surprised when he learned of Damir's suicide. Just like he said at the office, he knew a bitch ass nucca when he saw one and Damir's weak ass definitely fell into that category. But after his daughter was already growing up without a mother, Kaden was shocked that he would up and leave her in the world alone. That was selfish, but what could you expect from a bitch ass nucca.

"Babe," Kaden turned toward Naima, "What do you think?"

She was giving him that look. Hazel eyes melting Emerald ones.

"I think, you've already decided and only asking me as a formality." He said aiming his lopsided smile at her.

"I am not."

He raised his eyebrow cutting his eyes at her as she started laughing.

"Ok, ok, you're right. I want her and already have a vision of how to lay out her room," Coming up and wrapping her arms around him, "but I still want to know what you think. It's your home and life too, I know you said you would think about adopting, but God intervened and handed us a child."

Her imploring eyes were trying to reel him in and Kaden found himself sinking.

"Before we jump and make a rash decision, why don't we run it by the kids as well to see how they will feel about the whole situation?" He looked down at her, "What do you think?"

Naima nodded her head in agreement. "Talking to them about this may not be such a bad idea. But the decision is ultimately ours to make and I feel for that little angel, no Mommy and Daddy to love her."

"You're forgetting that she has a Grandmother that adores her. She is not alone in the world."

"I know, I know, but still, I want her with us."

Kaden shook his head and smiled. When Naima was dead set on something, she made it very clear how she felt.

"Ok Mocha, you got me. We can raise her."

Naima's face lit up like a Christmas tree. She was smiling as hard as she could as she threw her full body into Kaden's to hug and kiss him.

"Really baby? I'm so excited. We can tell the kids tonight!" Kaden laughed, so much for discussing with the kids prior to a decision being made.

The caseworker had re-entered the room, unnoticed by the couple a few moments before. Seeing him in the corner Naima's face turned red as she blushed from head to toe.

"I'm so sorry about the way we were behaving. We are more than thrilled to take Alanna." She clasped her hands together, "More than thrilled."

With them getting a new addition to the family, Kaden felt like it was now or never. He was anxious to share what he had been working on with Naima.

"Mocha, can you come in here for a moment?" He smiled when she slowly walked into the room with her overalls blotched with specks of paint. Her short hair was spiked on her head; she had colored paint freckling her face. He thought she looked adorable. She had wasted no time coming home and beginning to set up Alanna's room.

"Hey Babe." She said, stepping on tiptoe to give him a kiss, "What's going on?"

"I have a surprise for you."

"Kaden, I cannot handle anymore surprises in my life right now. I am officially surprised out." She said looking up at him; he had a little boy grin on his face and was pleading with those awesome eyes. She laughed, "Ok, you have me intrigued. What's the surprise?"

"I've been thinking it's time we do something for ourselves," bending on one knee in front of her he took out a ten-carat yellow diamond and grabbed her hand, "looking over the next hundred years of my life, I want you to be present in all of them. So if you're down for the cause, I was wondering if you would agree to be my wife," he paused for a beat, "again?" Kaden smiled as he winked at her.

Naima was really shocked, "baby, what in the wor— " He cut her off.

"Say yes."

Crying and smiling at the same time, Naima nodded, "Yes, of course I will."

Kaden placed the yellow diamond on her finger, pulling her into a hug before he devoured her mouth in a MTV worthy award winning best kiss.

After a minute Naima pulled back trying to catch her breath.

"Whoo, good thing we can't still get pregnant, cause tonight would definitely be a baby making night." She said.

Kaden laughed at her reaction, loving the fact that he could still turn her on so much with a simple kiss after so many years together.

"I love you." He said gazing into sun kissed Hazel eyes.

Naima couldn't help blushing from the way he was looking at her. "I love you too." She told him.

Sitting on the bed, pulling her into his lap Kaden continued to explain his intended surprise for her.

"I've planned for us to go to Fiji to renew our vows."

Naima's eyes widened as huge as saucers.

"Are you serious?"

"I'm very serious." He said as he kissed her on the cheek, "Everything is set up and ready for us. All we have to do is get on a plane and go."

"Oh my goodness, but how, when? Naima was a flabbergasted mess, "When did you have time to plan all of this?"

"Most of my late nights away from home; I was meeting with a planner who was helping me set up everything. The kids can come too if you like, or it can be just the two of us."

Leaning into his chest, Naima thought about that for a moment. "I think I would like the children to come. This would be a great memory for them to share with us and a new beginning for Alanna with our family."

"I was thinking the same thing. So how does next week sound?"

"What?" Naima's head swung around quickly to face him, "Babe, the kids are in school. I just went back to work; we cannot just take off next week unexpected like that."

"Mocha, you only live once, come on. The kids will love it," He began placing soft kisses on her neck, "You know you want to."

"Mmm, you know I can't think when you start doing that." She relaxed completely against him.

"That's the point." Kaden said as he lowered her overall straps. "I want you to say yes we'll go next week."

"Yes, yes." She said breathlessly, "We can go next week."

"That's all I wanted to hear."

He stood up with her in his arms and lowered her to the bed.

"Babe, I've been painting, let me take a shower first."

"No, I can play connect the dots. Now shhhh, no more talking, I want to enjoy pleasing my wife."

Chapter 16

The Qamea Resort in Fiji was absolutely breathtaking. Kaden had really out done himself, Naima couldn't help thinking. She looked over at her husband and laughed. All three kids were surrounding him. He'd picked up Alanna because Kalani kept trying to tickle her, she was now having a hiccup fit because she couldn't catch her breath from all the laughing she was doing. Namiyah was reaching around Alanna tickling her Dad's stomach, Naima continued to laugh, it really was a beautiful sight to see. Grabbing for the camera that was hidden in her purse she hurried to capture the moment on film. What was life without the fabulous memories to remember it by? Smiling as she continued to watch them, Naima was grateful for the way Namiyah and Kalani had taken to Alanna so quickly. She really was as cute as a button.

"Mommy, I want to go to the pool." Kalani said racing over to Naima. She guessed he was tired of tickle games.

"We have to get settled first, ok? Then you can go down to the pool." She told him.

"Okay."

"Some help while I was being attacked would have been nice." Kaden said as he walked over still carrying Alanna in his arms.

Naima couldn't keep the smile out of her voice, you seemed to have it all under control to me. I was rooting for you from afar."

Kaden snorted, "Those kids were trying to take me out. Three against one are never great odds."

"Oh hush. You survived. You looked mighty good too, fighting off three children. Sexiest thing I've ever seen in my life."

"Oh really?" He asked raising an eyebrow, "Guess I need to fight of children more often."

"Maybe." Naima smirked.

"He, he saved me from getting tickled by Kalani." Alanna stammered, giggling.

Taking her out of Kaden's arms to give a hug, "He sure did." Naima responded. Looking back over at Kaden, she asked, "What do we have planned for today?"

"I scheduled a day full of activities for the kids."

"And for us?" Naima inquired.

"For us I rented a private beach for the whole day. No kids, no interruptions, just us, the beach and God.

"Mmmm, that sounds like heaven. Just what the doctor ordered."

"He ordered more than that, just you wait."

Smiling softly, "I can only imagine." Switching back to Mommy mode, "Will the kids be fed during these activities and we are taking our cell phones in case something happens to one of them, right?"

"Don't you trust me woman?" Kaden asked her with a smile. "Of course the kids will be fed and yes you can bring your cell to the beach."

Naima breathed in a sigh of relief. "Ok good. And you know I trust you, you're my honey bunny, but I'm also a mom and dads be forgetting stuff sometimes."

"Touché Mocha, touché."

The private beach Kaden rented for them took Naima's breath away. This is exactly what she envisioned paradise would be like. The rainforest itself offered an enchanted mythical romantic setting. She was in love with Fiji. It had definitely been love at first sight, kind of how she felt about her boo Kaden.

Watching the emotions play across her face, Kaden knew Naima was in heaven. She had always been more of a tropical person loving the outdoors.

Naima knew Kaden was watching her take it all in, but behind her sunglasses she was also taking him in. After all these years, her man was still sexy beyond belief. He worked out constantly, which contributed to the eight pack stomach he had. Sometimes at night she would just run her fingers gently over the ripples. Exhaling a breath slowly, she was getting excited just thinking about it.

"It's beautiful isn't it?" He asked coming up behind her wrapping his arms around her waist.

"It's breathtaking." She whispered, "What's going on over there?" She asked pointing to the boat that had stopped on their beach.

"They're bringing us food for our picnic." Her face brightened,

"A picnic on the beach, how romantic." She smiled up at him, "You thought of everything huh?"

Kaden smiled down at her, "Anything for my Mochalatte." She laughed at that. He was a trip.

He grabbed her hand once the crew had everything set up and were retreating to their boat.

"Let's go partake in our lunch." He said.

"Let's!"

After they had eaten, Naima was stuffed beyond reason.

"Baby, oh my gosh." She moaned, "I am so embarrassed, I cannot believe I ate so much. My stomach hates me right now."

Kaden laughed at her dramatics, "Just rest baby, you'll be ok in a few minutes." He continued to chuckle as he looked at her sprawled across the blanket with her eyes closed. She was comical.

"Would you like a massage while you relax?"

Opening one eye, "A massage would be heavenly."

"Good, I just wanted an excuse to touch you. Roll onto your stomach for me"

"Baby, you never need an excuse to touch me. I always welcome my man's touch." Naima responded as she rolled over.

"Shh Mocha," Kaden said as he squeezed oil onto his hands and gently began kneading her back, "no talking, just enjoy my hands working over your body."

Naima did as he suggested and remained quiet as his hands worked their mojo on her body.

Feeling her body relax and lose all tenseness, Kaden began placing soft kisses down Naima's spine. Moaning softly as he gently kissed the side of her neck and lifted his hands to untie the strings on the back of her bikini she couldn't wait for him to get it off so she could feel his skin on hers. Slowly rolling her onto her back, he wasted no time working his mouth down to her hardened nipples. As he took one in his mouth Naima sucked in a quick breath and relished in the joy of the subtle flick of his tongue making her nipples even harder. Kneeling in front of her on the blanket, Kaden placed her legs on his shoulders, and began to kiss up her thigh.

Naima's moans echoed across the private beach as Kaden placed his head firmly between her legs and gently sucked on her clit. He seemed to know exactly how she liked it. Placing her hand on his head Naima couldn't help but moan louder as Kaden licked her up and down. She was getting closer to cumming and he knew it. The way he intensified his tongue strokes meant he could feel Naima's clit swelling and knew she would be yelling out any second. Grasping his head harder, Naima's legs started shaking as she felt her body's release taking over her. Kaden rose off the blanket knowing he had done his job and done it effectively.

Naima, realizing she had to get herself together, refused to let Kaden down. Trying to get up she noticed he was watching her with an amused grin.

"You feeling aight?"

She couldn't help but laugh, "I'm doing fine, thank you very much. Don't be laughing at me."

"I'm just saying, you were shaking and yelling kind of loud a moment ago. Walking may be too much for you right now."

"Oh, ok. I see you got jokes over there." Raising her eye brow and looking him dead in the eye "I got you."

Walking over to Kaden and running her hands down his arms, he willingly let Naima take over. His aura was intoxicating.

Naima wanted to lick him up and down and mount him as if she were riding in a derby.

Pressing up against Kaden's body to engage him in a kiss she gently sucked his bottom lip and could feel him responding to her. As he wrapped his arms around her, he placed his hands at the arch in her back and slowly trailed her curves with his fingertips. Sliding down the length of Kaden's body, Naima grabbed the waist of his shorts and pushed them to the floor. She was elated at his member springing out at her. Sitting on the blanket Indian style in front of Kaden she couldn't wait to put every inch of him in her mouth. Kissing the tip before she slowly guided him into her mouth, Naima was savoring every bit of him. Using both hands as she sucked and ran her hands up and down his shaft she could feel him pulsating on her tongue. Hearing him moan audibly as he put his hands in her short hair and began to push her head up and down he said her name as he was nearing his peak. Moving quickly, Naima pulled him down to the blanket so she could straddle Kaden and slowly slid her tight, wetness on top of him. Upon entering her, Kaden could no longer contain himself, "Damn, this shit is good."

Smiling to herself Naima proceeded to ride Kaden as if her life depended on it. Giving in to Naima's look and feel, Kaden could feel control slipping away. Gripping Naima's waist he helped to slid her up and down on top of him. Feeling the end in sight Kaden caught her mouth in a kiss and released himself into Paradise.

Waking up the next morning with a smile on her face, Naima was still thinking about her romantic day with Kaden. Glancing over at him sleeping, she reached over and placed a kiss on the tip of his nose. Lord knows she loved that man. Saddened by the fact she had to get out of the bed and leave him, she threw the comforter back and got up quietly. They were renewing their wedding vows today and she was elated, but before she could worry about herself, she had to get three children up and moving.

Retrieving a robe from the closet she put it on in preparation to go to the kids suite. A knock on the door interrupted her. Moving swiftly to open it so Kaden wasn't disturbed, she was surprised to see an older lady standing there.

"Yes?" She asked.

"Hi, I'm Rosa, your event planner for today and we must get moving yes, yes."

Naima smiled. Rosa reminded her so much of her mother that it was hilarious. She stepped completely in the hall and closed the door behind her.

"Nice to meet you Rosa. I'm up. I was about to wake the kids to get them ready."

"Oh no, no. Kids are up and bathing, getting ready. My staff has taken care of it. We worry about you now. Into shower you go, then hair and make-up. I'll be back in half hour to get you. You'll be ready? Yes?" She said as she turned and walked away.

"Yes Ma'am." Naima yelled behind her.

The ceremony started promptly at 3:00 p.m. Rosa was not having it, everything was in perfect order and Naima could not have been more appreciative of Rosa and her team of workers. Because of them she hadn't had to worry about the children at all. They were all taken care of and she for one grateful. It had been nice to only worry about herself for once.

Kaden had truly gone above and beyond himself. Their vow renewal was taking place in the middle of the rainforest. It was almost too good to be true, like a fairytale. The kids were all there to witness and Naima couldn't have been more excited. She had chosen to wear a simple one-shoulder crepe dress by Vera Wang. It was mermaid style, perfectly appropriate for a mystical ceremony such as this one. It made her feel incredibly feminine.

Making her way through the forest to the ceremony site at Rosa's command, Naima's eyes lit up when she arrived, her mother, and Kaden's parents were standing there. The only thing that would have been better was if her Dad had been here to walk her down the aisle. Eyes misting a little, she paused to get herself together, then slowly began the walk with the violinists playing softly on the side. Seeing Kaden standing at the front waiting for her made life fabulous and all was right with the world.

Kaden fell in love with Naima all over again at the first sight of her in all white. His Mocha was beautiful. Trying his best not to tear up himself, he sent a quick prayer up to God, "Thank you for choosing this wonderful woman to be my wife and share my life with me. You did a great job and I'll never be able to thank you enough. Amen. In his heart he swore he heard "You're welcome."

Reaching the front where Kaden was waiting for her, she put her hand in his and smiled into his eyes.

"You ready to pledge eternity to me again?"

"I was ready the first time," He said smiling down at her as he laced their fingers together, "I willing pledge my life to you for the second time, so you know I really mean it, for eternity and beyond. You are my one and only and I will love you for always."

After witnessing Naima and Kaden's vow renewal ceremony in FiJi and being surrounded by their undying love for one another, Cynthia was finally ready to forgive Kenneth and talk to Coleen. Naima and Kaden had been through so much and their love had let them survive it all. If Kenneth were still alive, who knows if theirs would have survived or not, but she couldn't let his son suffer because of the crazy mistakes adults make.

Picking up the phone and dialing the number before she lost her nerve, Cynthia waited for Coleen to pick up.

"Hello."

"Hello Coleen. It's Cynthia Vaughn."

Coleen was shocked. Cynthia was actually calling her. "Hi Cynthia. What can I do for you today?" She asked trying to play it cool.

Taking a deep breath, Cynthia pressed on, "I was hoping we could talk about the best thing to do for Justin and that's it."

Coleen didn't respond. She was afraid to say anything that would change Cynthia's mind, so she waited patiently for her to continue.

Cynthia didn't know what to make of Coleen's silence so she forged ahead, "I am putting a third of Kenneth's insurance money into a trust fund for Justin to receive when he turns twenty-one. You will also receive five thousand dollar monthly payments on behalf of the Vaughn's until Justin turns eighteen. That brings your total to sixty thousand dollars a year and two million in his trust fund. Does this seem fair to you?"

Once again Coleen was shocked. "It is more than fair." Coleen said, finally finding her voice, "Thank you so much for this."

"Don't thank me Chile. Thank the Lord above. Have a nice day." Cynthia said as she hung up the phone. Now her soul could rest a little easier. She needed to handle that situation for her own piece of mind.

"How was Fiji? I'm so jealous."

"You should be girl, you should be." Naima laughed.

"You just going to rub it in my face huh?"

"I sure am." Naima said waving her right hand at Haven.

"OH MY GOD! That is one huge yellow diamond!" Haven said grabbing her hand and bringing it closer so she could inspect it further.

"What can I say. My man loves me." Naima said with a smile as the memories from FiJi danced in her head.

"Yeah, he does." Haven agreed. She, Naima and Kadir were strolling through the park waiting for the kids to get out of practice.

"Why do you have sunglasses on and it looks like it's going to be raining in a little bit?"

Haven shrugged as she pushed the stroller, "Didn"t feel like putting on make-up today."

"Huh?" Naima was confused, "Girl, you rarely wear make-up, what you talking about? Don't forget who you talking to, don't be lying to me."

"Ok, alright," Haven huffed removing her glasses, "I just didn't want people staring at me ok."

Naima gasped when she saw Haven's face, she had two black eyes. Stopping short she pulled Haven into her arms.

"You have to go to the police. You cannot continue to let Chris do this to you!" Looking Haven in her eyes, "I thought you told me he wasn't hitting you anymore. When did this start back up?"

Putting her glasses back on her face, Haven whispered, "When Camille died. He hasn't been the same since then. I think he's going through a depression or something. It's not his fault."

"Don't you dare try to explain his behavior. This is unacceptable. He cannot get away with this. Why didn't you tell me what was going on?

Continuing to push Kadir's stroller through the park Haven replied, "Because I knew you would react like this."

Grabbing Haven by the arm, "Honey," Naima said looking her dead in the eye, "this is not ok. Chris is not ok. He needs help and I mean real help. You should not have to take this type of abuse. My mom has plenty of space in that big house of hers, why not take the kids and stay there?" Naima pleaded with her, "Please, I don't want to see anything bad happen to you. These types of situations always end badly."

Looking into Naima's worried face Haven agreed, "Ok, I'll call your mom and we'll see about moving me and the kids there."

Naima wasn't convinced, but she couldn't force her to do anything she didn't want to do.

Chapter 17

Haven had given serious thought to Naima's offer, but she knew Chris would never allow her to take his sons and move out. It just would not happen in this lifetime. She didn't know how much longer she could operate under this strain though. Chris was trying to break her down physically, mentally and emotionally. He didn't care anymore, his eyes told her that. Before he at least pretended to care, now all she saw was pure hatred and that's what scared her the most.

"Chris, what would you like for dinner?"

"I won't be here, do what you want."

Haven sighed with relief. Good, that meant tonight she would be able to rest easy. Besides Naima was coming over. She seemed to want to come over a lot more frequently these days. Haven knew it was because she was genuinely concerned about her and since she hadn't spoken to her family in years, Naima was the only family she had besides Chris and their kids.

By the time Naima arrived, Haven had dinner all laid out.

"Girl, who you call yourself feeding? It's just me and Alanna tonight.

"Oh, where are Kalani and Namiyah?"

Naima grabbed plates for she and Alanna, "Namiyah said she had some research to do or something and Kalani and Kaden are home playing Madden. Neither of them are moving for a few hours."

"Thanks for coming over and keeping me company. Kaven is at a friends and Kadir is sleeping hs little heart away. Giving Mommy some much needed chill time. Yes!"

Naima laughed as she made sure Alanna was all situated. "I don't know what chill time is like. With another little one in the house, I'm a busy bee."

"Speaking of kids, I've been meaning to ask a favor of you, you know if something were to happen to me."

Naima cut her eyes at her, "What would happen to you?"

"I don't know, I'm just saying if something were to happen to me, will you take Kaven and Kadir in?"

That stopped Naima from making her plate completely. She immediately put the plate down and grabbed Haven's face. "Don't you talk like that. Nothing is going to happen to you. Do you hear me? I will not allow it."

Tears began escaping Haven's eyes, "Please Naima, tell me if something happens to me you'll look after them. I need to know they'll be taken care of just in case."

Pulling Haven into a hug, Naima was really afraid this time. "Of course I'll look after them. You know you don't even need to ask that."

"Thank you." Haven said returning Naima's hug with all the love in her heart, because she knew Naima meant it.

Naima didn't know what to expect anymore. It seemed like everyone's life was spiraling out of control and no one was trying to seek any help. With all this chaos going on, she had thought about seeing a therapist herself. But after the Coleen fiasco, she could honestly say that she no longer trusted therapists either. Who knew the world could be such a dishonest place? You could trust almost no one.

"Baby."

"Oh,oh. I can tell from your tone that this is about to be a long discussion."

"Hush silly. Not long just deep."

"Figured."

"Kaden."

"Sorry Baby, I'm listening. Give it to me."

"I kind of told Haven tonight that if something happened to her we would take care of her kids."

Kaden groaned inwardly a little. "Does she plan on something happening to her?"

"I don't know. She and Chris are really going through it. She scared me tonight. I've never been scared before. I think she needs to leave that situation completely. Chris is eventually going to kill her. You should have seen her the other day when we were at the park. Both of her eyes had been blackened."

"I don't think you should hang around her as much. Because if you get caught in a situation between the two of them and Chris puts his hands on you, Imma have to put that nucca six feet under."

Naima placed a kiss on Kaden's cheek. "Baby, nothing will happen to me, promise and I can't stay away from Haven right now. I'm too worried about her. She doesn't tell me anything anymore, so who knows what's really going on with her."

"Ok Mocha. I trust your judgment. Let me know if you need me to do anything."

Naima shook her head, "Nope there's nothing. I just wanted you on notice about the kid thing."

"Ok, I have officially been notified. Let's pray that we'll never need to mention this notice again."

"Agreed."

Tyson hung up the phone and smiling at his expression in the mirror. Things were going nicely, he couldn't have hoped for a better outcome to his plan. Hearing the doorbell chime, he gave himself one last glance over before letting Emeri in. They were having a date night, pizza and movies.

Opening the door, his breath caught. He was always taken back by how beautiful Emeri was. The big crinkly hair with the light eyes were enough to make any man pause and stare. Too bad she was half crazy, if it weren't for that one thing, she would be perfect.

"Hi gorgeous."

"Hi." She said walking in past him with a bag in her arms.

"What you got in the bag?" He asked as he shut the door.

"Wine." She said pulling out a bottle. "Did you order pizza already?"

"I did."

"Good, buffalo wings too right?"

"Yes," he said taking the wine from her. "I got you covered."

"You're way too good to me."

Tyson smiled at that. "Woman, go into the room and pick out

a movie for us to watch."

"Ok." She replied as she went down into the basement to make a selection.

Tyson had always marveled at the human psyche, that's probably why he choose to be a psychiatrist in the first place.

There were times like now when Emeri seemed so normal, but her mood could shift so quickly. Sometimes he wondered what would happen if he were to break things off with her. What would she do? Would his life be in danger or not. Something told him it would be, so he opted not to think about it to much.

Uncorking the wine, pouring them each a glass, he took the bottle and the glasses down to the basement. He came back up to answer the door when the pizza man arrived.

Once they were all settled in the basement with wine, pizza, buffalo wings and a blanket, Tyson asked Emeri to press play on the DVD player so that date night could officially begin.

Hearing the opening to "Why Did I Get Marrried?" By Tyler Perry, Tyson wondered why she had chosen this particular movie.

"Any reason for the movie choice?"

"I heard Tyler Perry was a good Writer and Director, so I wanted to see first hand if it were true or not." Emeri said right before she stuffed a slice of pizza in her mouth.

"Cool."

Sitting back, allowing her to enjoy the movie, Tyson didn't say much of anything until the credits began to roll.

"So, what did you think?"

"I think he had some very memorable characters. I liked the movie a lot. I gues what people have been saying about him is true."

"Yeah, I like it ok."

Tyson began to clean up the remnants of their evening.

"Hey," Emeri started, interrupting the silence, "I've been thinking about this whole situation with Namiyah and I've come to the conclusion that I believe she knows too much."

Just that quick, Tyson could tell that sane Emeri was being replaced by insane Emeri. Continuing to clean up, Tyson waited for her to go on.

"I may have to do something to ensure she keeps quiet."

"Something like what?" He asked softly.

"I haven't decided yet, but whatever it is it has to be untraceable."

"Emeri, I don't know about this. Namiyah is only fifteen and your niece. Maybe you should ease up on her just a little."

Emeri stopped cleaning up to look at him. Suddenly suspicious, she felt like she couldn't trust him.

"Are you taking up for her?"

"No I'm not. All I'm saying is she's a little girl. Don't go doing anything drastic. She's a child, is all I'm saying and your family has been through enough."

"My family is dead!" Emeri yelled throwing the blankets she'd just picked up back on the floor. "Those people are not my family. I have no one."

Tyson put the pizza boxes on the table and went to console Emeri. Outbursts were good. At least she was reacting and showing emotion. It was when she gave no reaction he bacame worried.

Attempting to run his fingers through her massive curls, he gave up in defeat and opted to rub her back instead.

Pulling back out of his reach, Emeri grabbed her things. She needed to get away from Tyson so she could think. She didn't know if she trusted him anymore.

"I have to go."

"Already?"

"Yes. Now. Good-bye." And she stormed out.

Tyson was left trying to figure out what he had done wrong.

Chapter 18

Naima woke out of her sleep suddenly drenched in sweat. A bad feeling washed over her. Something wasn't right she could feel it. Looking over at Kaden she saw that he was still sleeping peacefully. Glancing at the red digital numbers, she read 1:23 on the clock. Rising to check on the kids, Naima went to all three bedrooms and all three children were sound asleep. She wanted to call her mom, but knew if she phoned this late her mom would automatically think that something was wrong. So she decided to lay back down, but she did so with a heavy heart. Something was not right in the world.

The phone ringing woke her up this time. The digital clock read 5:21. Picking up the receiver slowly, Naima braced herself for bad news. All her children were home, so the only reason she would be getting a call this early in the morning was if something happened to her mother or Haven.

"Hello."

"May I speak to Naima Fairchild please?"

"This is she."

Kaden sat up slowly and mouthed, "Is everything ok?"

"Ma'am we need you to come down, to the fifth precinct to pick up Kaven and Kadir Thomas. If you do not come for them we have no choice but to turn them over to Child Protective Services."

"Can you tell me what's going on please?"

"Ma'am we would prefer not to divulge information over the phone. Will you be coming to collect the children?"

"Yes of course. I'll be right down." Hanging up the phone, Naima got up immediately.

"What's going on?" Kaden asked.

"Come on, put your clothes on. We have to go down to the station and pick up Kaven and Kadir or they're going to turn them over to Child Protective Services."

"Does this mean what I think it means?" Kaden asked as he got up to put his clothes on.

"I have no idea what's going on. I'm afraid to know. They are going to tell us when we get there." Naima threw her sneakers on and pulled a sweatshirt out of the drawer. "Babe I'm going to go in and let Namiyah know that we need to run not and to watch Kalani and Alanna."

"Aight. I'll go heat up the car."

"Ok, Baby."

Going into the precinct, Naima was afraid of what she would find out. Showing the proper identification, she and Kaden were taken to a back room where Kaven and Kadir were being held.

"Running up to her immediately, Kaven threw his arms around her waist and wouldn't let go. Kaden picked up a sleeping Kadir and placed the six-month-old bay in Naima's waiting arms.

"You go find out what's going on. I'll stay in here with the kids." She told him .

Kaden nodded and followed the officer out the room.

Rubbing Kaven's back, Naima focused her attention on her Godson. "Hey munchkin, you doing ok?" Looking at his face she could tell he had been crying.

Shaking his head, no he continued to hug her and she felt his grip tighten. "It'll be ok. Your God Mommy is here to take care of everything ok?"

"Mmmmhmmn." He sniffed never looking up. Kaden came back into the room then and took Kadir out of Naima's arms and put him into his car seat, then looked over at Naima and said, "Time for us to go."

They rode home in silence, each confined to their own thoughts.

"Kaven honey, you go ahead in your normal room you stay in and I'll come in, shortly to check on you. I'm sure this was a long night and you're tired."

"Ok." He said sadly, as he walked down the hall.

As she and Kaden walked into their room with Kadir, Naima needed answers for her questions.

"So babe what did they say? What happened?"

Kaden began taking his clothes off slowly his back was to Naima and he wanted to take his time with responding.

"Kaden Fairchild!" Naima raised her voice slightly, "What is going on? You better tell me something right now!"

Turning around to face her, he braced himself for her reaction, "Seems like your worst fears have come true, Chris strangled Haven to death sometime this morning."

Naima sat on the bed. 1:23 this morning she thought, that's when Haven breathed her last breath, she just knew it. She had known something was wrong. She should have called Haven; maybe she would be alive now.

"I knew this was going to happen." Naima placed her face in her hands, "I told you last time I was there she scared me."

Coming to her side of the bed kneeling in front of her Kaden honestly didn't know what to say. He just offered his support.

"Why do bad things keep happening all around us? "Naima asked as she threw her arms around his neck.

Enclosing her in a hug, Kaden gently wiped the tears from her eyes.

"I don't know Mocha."

"I can't keep going through this. At some point, life has to get better. We are burying too many people back to back. I'm tired of going to funerals. I've been to enough to last me a lifetime.

"I know Baby."

Naima was grateful for Kaden. There was no way she would have been able to make it through the last five years of her life without him. He was her blessing. She'd be lost without him.

After checking in on Kaven to make sure he was all settled in and taken care of. Naima rejoined Kaden in their room. They seriously had to have a talk.

"Baby, we need to talk."

"About all these children I presume."

"How did you guess?"

Shrugging Kaden responded, "Process of elimination."

"Well for starters, I had no idea that in a few weeks our household of four would jump to seven. We now have a six month old in the house."

Smiling slowly, "You did say you wanted more children. Now you have a whole house full."

"That's one way of looking at the bright side, if there was bright side to this whole sordid situation." Dropping her head down her eyes misted, "I cannot believe Haven is gone, feels like only yesterday we were shopping at the mall for Louis Vuitton baby bags and now I have the baby bag, the baby, and no her."

"Come on Mocha. You have to be strong for the children."

"I know. It's just too much you know . One family shouldn't go through so much."

"Baby, we'll survive. We always do."

"You're right." Naima took a deep breath as she wiped her eyes.

"I'm ok now. I just had to get it out my system so I could get myself together." Breathing in slowly she jumped up, "Ok, I'm ready. Let me go downstairs and make these kids breakfast, then call my momma and let her know about the change of events." She gave Kaden a kiss on the cheek, grabbed Kadir who was still sleeping in his car seat and bounded out the room and down the stairs.

Kaden shook his head and grinned. He loved that woman, she was definitely a trooper. You might catch her off guard for a second, but she rebounded like no one's business. That was his Mocha for you. God had truly broken the mold when he made her.

Emeri walked past the sitting room and smiled at Namiyah. Namiyah ignored her. All the new distractions at her parents house offered her plenty of alone time to sort things out about her Aunt. Things had not gotten better between them. Namiyah could tell that Emeri knew she knew who had caused the fire at Camille's house killing her Granddaddy. She had been getting bad vibes from Emeri, not that she didn't always have bad vibes around her psycho Aunt anyway, but lately she could tell through their interactions that something was going on. The reason she knew that was because Emeri was making it a point to interact with her. Namiyah knew better though. Her Momma wasn't raising no fool. She wouldn't trust Emeri if they were the last two people on Earth. She would just have to befriend the dolphins or some other animal before that took place.

Sitting at her Gram's house, she thought about her home life. It seemed like home was in an uproar lately. Alanna, Kaven and Kadir were all moved in with them. Namiyah found herself excited to have a new little sister and a new baby in the house. She was used to Kaven always being there, so that was normal anyway.

The funeral for his mom had been sad. Namiyah had never seen her mother so distraught. Not even when she was in the hospital recovering or when she learned, she wouldn't be able to have any more children. She had always held it together. Haven's funeral was another story however. They had been friends since they were kids themselves, must be hard to bury someone you have known your whole life. Good thing the house was full of kids now to keep her mom's spirit's up. Namiyah could tell her mother loved taking care of all of them and Namiyah loved her for that. She wouldn't trade her mom for anyone in the world.

"Namiyah."

"Yes, Gram." She sighed as her thoughts were interrupted.

"Can you go to the basement and get Kalani's old play pen out? It should be buried in the back closet somewhere."

"Yes Ma'am."

Making her way to the basement, Namiyah began searching through closets. Her Gram didn't tell her exactly which back closet had the play pen in it. This basement had plenty of closets. Beginning at the first one she came to, Namiyah was shocked to see an old collection of guns, knives and swords in this one. This must have been Granddaddy's thing because she couldn't imagine Gram having anything to do with any of this stuff.

The light from the closet caught the glare of something in the corner. Reaching over thoughtfully, Namiyah pulled it out of the corner and her eyes grew about three sizes. She was holding a real life machete. She had seen pictures of one before, but she had never gotten the opportunity to hold one before.

"Namiyah! Where is the play pen?" Her Gram yelled from the top of the steps.

"Sorry Gram. I'm still looking."

Hurrying to put the machete back in its place, Namiyah backed out of that closet to find the play pen before Gram made it down the steps herself to look for it, which would not be a good thing. Making a mental note of where the machete was placed in case she needed it for future use, she found the playpen and went back upstairs.

Chapter 19

Coleen couldn't have been more thrilled. Plans had been set and things were finally being put into motion. She was almost giddy at the arrangements that had been made.

Ever since her practicing license had been suspended pending a review from the Licensing Board, there really hadn't been any real joy in her life outside of her baby, Justin. After their fight at the Vaughn house, Emeri had made it a point to destroy her life by telling Coleen's job about an inappropriate relationship between she and Kenneth. As if killing Coleen's sister and father of her child weren't good enough, Emeri had to take her job too. Coleen could care less if she had proof to back up her statement, she knew Emeri was responsible for Camille and Kenneth's death's. Justice would be paid. Coleen was going to see to it.

Chris was more upset with himself for ending up behind bars again than he was with anyone else. He'd vowed to himself that he would never come back to this place and yet here he was. Both times had been on account of Haven. He knew he wouldn't be getting out this time. They were going to throw away the key on his ass this time.

"Aye," the guard said coming to unlock his cell, "you have a visitor."

Following the guard down the hall to the visiting area, Chris was trying to imagine who would be coming to see him.

Taking a seat in front of the glass in his designated area, he was surprised to see Coleen sitting on the other side. She picked up the phone pointing her finger at his indicating that he should do the same.

"How are you holding up in here?" she asked him.

"As good as can be expected. What are you doing here?"

"I figured I'd stop by to see you to ask what the hell happened? You were the guy asking me to wait for the authorities to handle Camille and Kenneth's case and then you turn around and get locked up on murder charges." Coleen was looking at Chris through the glass as if he were crazy.

Chris shrugged, "I don't know. I snapped. She told me she was taking Kaven and Kadir and moving out. I told her I would never allow her to take my children away from me. Then she told me that she was going down to the station to file a report of abuse and my black ass was going back to jail," he shrugged again, "to much alcohol, to much hatred in our situation, all I remember is coming to with my hands around her neck. I don't even recall choking her." Shaking his head side to side in disbelief, "I tried to perform CPR on her, but it was too late. She was already gone."

"Time's up." The guard said.

After leaving the jail, Coleen picked Justin up and took him to the park. Watching him play with the other kids, she was beyond emotional. Her little boy was getting so big so fast. She remembered the night she and Kenneth had brought him home from the hospital. He was a mirror image of his Dad. She was so sad Kenneth wouldn't be around to see the kind of man that he would one day become.

Watching Justin play, Coleen took a moment to reminisce about Kenneth. She remembered the first time he had stayed behind after one of Emeri's therapy sessions to ask her if she thought Emeri could really be helped. She had been in a rush to eat that day because she had scheduled appointments back to back the entire day. So she had taken it upon herself to invite him to dinner so they could discuss Emeri, he had agreed. Through the course of dinner is when she'd come to see how the situation was truly grieving him.

He'd needed someone to talk too, she had been available to lend an ear. Soon, after each of Emeri's sessions they would accompany each other to dinner afterwards and that began the makings of their beautiful relationship. Coleen was no fool however, she knew he would never leave Cynthia. She and Kenneth never discussed it because Coleen never felt the need to bring it up. She knew her place.

The only serious life decision they'd made with one another was Justin. Coleen was getting older and had wanted a child. Kenneth was hesitant at first, but she had been able to talk him into it and once they found out they were having a boy, Kenneth was very excited. He had always wanted a boy, so she'd helped his wish to come true.

Breaking her attention away from Justin for a moment, her mind wondered back to Chris. She truly felt bad for him. She knew he hadn't been the same since Camille's death. She wasn't sure if he would survive in jail this time, grief had began to slowly kill him. His spirit had already died of a broken heart. If Camille hadn't died, who knows what would and wouldn't be. Coleen blamed Emeri, inadvertently she was responsible for destroying so many lives. How could one person hold so much power? Up until this point, Emeri had been a lucky girl, but luck was funny like that, eventually it ran out.

All would have been fine too, if Camille had never slipped and told Emeri about Coleen and Kenneth. Once that mishap happened, everything began to go down hill, which is why everyone's life was now screwed up. If Emeri was good at nothing else, she was defintely a master at destroying lives.

Tyson knew he and Emeri's time had come to an end. Ever since their movie night her whole demeanor towards him had changed. As a therapist, he was trained to identify the warning signs and Emeri had warning signs all around her.

He looked down as his cell vibrated on his hip.

"Hello." He said into the phone.

"Hi. Everything is in place. Two days."

"Good. Two days it is." He said disconnecting from the call.

Naima was tired. The new change of events in her life with all these children and their schedules was taking a toll on her. Their social calendar was more packed then hers. She loved them all and they were definitely a joy to be around, she was just exhausted from how quickly she had gotten thrown into a three ring circus and how she was forced to adjust. Kaden had been a huge help. Naima was so grateful. Unlike when Kalani was born, Kaden was getting up in the middle of the night if Kadir cried and if any of the rest of the kids were having issues with anything, he was right there to help. Her mom was doing a great job as well. Since Naima couldn't take so much leave since she had just gone back to work and Kaden had picked up a consultant gig, her mom had stepped in to watch Kadir during the day and pick up Alanna from half day kindergarten. It all worked out perfectly.

More than anything Naima was happy that Namiyah seemed to stop worrying herself to death about Emeri. She could tell they hadn't called a truce, but at least her baby girl was no longer torturing herself about it. They hadn't had any more discussions recently so Naima was happy, all seemed all right in the world now or whatever world was left after the numerous deaths they had experienced recently.

Emeri was done with Tyson. She could tell that something was going on with him. Ever since their date night, something hadn't been right. It really sucked for him because now he would have to be disposed of; he knew entirely too much information about her and the things she had done.

This time Emeri didn't have a 'can do' attitude about Tyson. She had really hoped that they would have been able to make it work. She should have known better. Happiness wasn't for her. She understood that now. Life was meant to be played like a game. Whoever had the better strategy succeeded at the game of life, no more, no less.

Between Tyson and Namiyah, she had her work cut out for her. There was no way she could do anything drastic right now; it would look too suspicious coming right after Camille and Kenneth's incident. The authorities would definitely know that it was an inside job at the center.

"What to do, what to do?" She thought. She had already threatened Namiyah, but she couldn't be sure if that had worked or not. The way that girl was always looking at her, Emeri wanted to stick her foot out and let her fall down the stairs and break her neck or something, anything to break that haughty attitude.

Emeri was already killing Namiyah with kindness. She could see her little teenage brain's wheels turning. Hopefully, she was smart enough to bow out gracefully. Emeri knew she was much better at this game than Namiyah would ever be. Emeri had to hand it to Namiyah though; the girl really had a lot of heart. If Namiyah wouldn't have waged a full on battle with her from jump, Emeri honestly would have liked the girl for what it was worth. Shoot, she did like her; Emeri saw a lot of herself in Namiyah. Too bad, it wouldn't save her, but she at least at the end of the day could say that she respected her.

Looking around her room, she felt like she was confined. Ever since everyone in the universe had entrusted their kids to Naima, Ma Cyn's house seemed more like a day care than a peaceful serenity. She hated it. There were children everywhere. Every time she turned around, she was tripping over one of those little bastards. It was sickening. The only one she showed the least bit of interest in was Kadir. She never let people know this, but she loved babies. The idea of having one had crossed her mind a time or two, but she couldn't trust men enough to get to that point. The one candidate that would have been perfect turned out to be a fraud. Which was fine, she wasn't built for dating anyway. After the episode with Damir and then learning that he committed suicide, Emeri was glad she had decided not to pursue him. Who wanted a man that would kill himself? Everything about that screamed of weakness. She was mad at herself for being attracted to him in the first place.

Her thoughts shifted back to Tyson, there had to be a way to get rid of him without drawing heat down on herself. Unexplainable accidents happened every day. A slow smile spread across Emeri's face. She had just thought of the perfect solution.

Chapter 20

Namiyah crept up to Emeri's room. It was now or never, she knew her Aunt, if she attempted to do what she planned and didn't succeed, Emeri would come back for her and kill her. "It's going to be her or me and I refuse to be the one." She thought to herself.

Knocking and listening at Emeri's door before she opened it, she didn't hear any movement. Knowing that Gram would be back in about two hours from the park with Kalani, Kaven, Alanna, and Kadir, Namiyah wasn't that worried about time.

Pushing the door open slowly, Namiyah was surprised to see Emeri's normally neat and organized room in such disarray. It seemed as if she must have been looking for something, had gotten frustrated and threw everything everywhere. Stepping back, pulling the door shut Namiyah began to get a little nervous. Where was Emeri? She was supposed to be in her room. Her car was outside and Gram had said she was upstairs before she left. Emeri had to be in the bathroom she figured. Creeping slowly down the hall trying her best to avoid the squeaky floorboards,

Namiyah finally made it to the end of the hall unnoticed. She was ready to get down to the dirty deed and move on.

Seeing the light coming from the bathroom, she pulled the machete her Granddad had kept in the basement from behind her back. She was going to slice her dear Auntie into bits and pieces, grill her up and feed her to the neighbor's dogs, bones and all. Namiyah had never hated anyone as much as she did Emeri.

The bathroom door was slightly ajar. Pushing it all the way open with her foot, Namiyah dropped the machete in shock. Emeri's lifeless eyes stared back at her. The mirror in the bathroom had been shattered and a single solitary piece stuck out from Emeri's throat. Half of her body was in the bathtub and the other half was on the linoleum floor. The only way her body could be angled in such a fashion was if her back was broken and a bone was sticking out of her left leg as if she'd fallen and broken it.

Namiyah saw blood splattered everywhere. Looking down at her shoe, she noticed she had stepped in some. Disgusted with the whole thing she removed her shoe and entered the bathroom completely. She had to get the blood off her shoe so she didn't track it through the house.

Taking another look at Emeri, she was upset that someone had beat her to the punch, but happy that she was gone. The world was a better place without her in it. Preparing to leave the bathroom once she finished cleaning off her shoe, Namiyah picked up the machete, no point in leaving it there for someone to find, they may think she had something to do with this mess.

Opening the door, she jumped back when she saw Gram standing directly in front of the door.

"Chile, what in the world happened to Emeri's room?"

Nervously, Namiyah tried to block the sight inside the bathroom with her body.

"I don't know Gram," she tried changing the subject, "What are ya'll doing back so early? I thought you would be gone for a while."

"Kalani left his basketball so we had to come back." Giving her a hard look, Cynthia sensed she was hiding something. "What have you been doing?" she asked her suspiciously.

"Oh, nothing." Namiyah wondered if she looked as guilty as she felt. In all actuality she really shouldn't feel guilty, she didn't do anything."

"Really?" Cynthia wasn't convinced, "What are you hiding behind your back?"

Namiyah knew if he owned up to the machete she would have to own up to what happened in the bathroom and she had nothing to do with that, so she remained quiet.

"Namiyah, I am not playing with you. Move out the way, you're hiding something."

"No I'm not Gram, honest."

"Move out the way now. And where is Emeri?"

Grudgingly moving out of the bathroom doorway Namiyah began explaining immediately.

"I didn't do it. I found her that way."

Cynthia gave her a funny look, "Found what, what way?" she asked as she walked into the bathroom and stopped short. Turning back to face Namiyah she screamed, "What did you do?"

"I did— "

"Why would you do this to her?" Cynthia screamed before grabbing Namiyah by the shoulders so hard that the machete fell out of her hands to the floor. Eyes opening even wider, "What are you doing with that?" Cynthia asked her with tears streaming down her face, "This family has been through enough, how could you do this?"

"Gram," Namiyah kept trying to explain as her own tears fell, "I didn't do it believe me."

"What ya'll doing up here? Gram I found my ball, you ready to go?"

"Kalani," Cynthia said sharply, "Go back downstairs and call 911 for Gram. Tell them to come quickly and you and the rest of the kids go play in the basement ok. Tell them I said so."

"911." Kalani repeated confused.

"Yes baby, go call now ok. Be Gram's helper, I need you today."

"Ok." he bounded down the stairs to do as he was told.

Namiyah tried again to plead her case, "Gram listen, I found her that way."

"If that were true why do you have blood on you?"

Looking down, Namiyah saw blood on her shirt. She must have brushed up on something when she was cleaning her shoe.

Glancing back at Gram sheepishly, "I know this looks bad, but I had nothing to do with it, I swear."

Cynthia stared Namiyah dead in her eyes, "Then what is your Grandfather's machete doing up here."

Good question, Namiyah thought. "I was looking at it."

"Looking at it in the same room the Aunt you hate is dead in? I find that hard to believe."

"Gram!" Kalani yelled up the stairs, "They are on the way."

"Thanks baby. Can you bring me the phone? I need to call your mother." Cynthia closed the bathroom door behind her so he couldn't see inside.

Racing up the stairs he shook his head, "No you don't, she and Daddy just pulled up outside."

"Good." Grabbing Namiyah's arm Cynthia practically dragged her down the steps, if Namiyah hadn't been paying attention she would have fallen.

"You sit on that couch right there and don't you move." Cynthia said as she pushed Namiyah onto the couch.

Naima was all smiles when she and Kaden walked into her mother's house to pick up their five kids. It still amazed her how she had gone from two children to five children within a matter of weeks and the sad circumstances that had brought them all to her. She had always wanted a house full of children, just not the way she had gotten them but she loved them all just the same.

Her mother met her at the door with a tear streaked face and red eyes. Naima's smile instantly vanished; she knew immediately that something was very wrong. Cynthia Vaughn wouldn't be caught dead looking like this, so whatever was going on was major.

"Ma, what's wrong?" Not hearing the kids usual noisy chatter, she became worried, "Are the kids ok? Where is everyone?"

Her mom was still standing at the door not saying a word.

"I'll go look around." Kaden said as he walked past Naima and her mother. He could tell by looking at Ms. Cynthia that something was up.

Naima watched Kaden walk off then focused her attention back on her mother.

"Mommy, tell me what's wrong. This isn't like you."

"Chile," Cynthia brought her gaze up to meet Naima's, "Namiyah done gone and killed Emeri. I walked in on her finishing the job."

Naima felt her whole body go numb. There was no way Namiyah would do something like that, no way at all. Backing away from her mother, her own maternal instincts kicked in. Naima was outraged.

"How could you accuse your own grandchild of such a thing? I know my child and she would not do this."

Cynthia looked at Naima as if she were delusional. She loved her child but naivety should only go but so far.

"Excuse me Missy, you mind your manners. I am not a liar and I'm still your mother."

"Mother or no mother, I'm not minding any manners, you are accusing my child of murder and I will not stand for it!"

"I told you, I saw it with my own eyes."

Naima narrowed her eyes in anger, "You're going to stand here and tell me you watched Namiyah murder Emeri and didn't do anything to prevent it? I don't believe you. That doesn't make a lick of sense."

"I mean, I walked in when she was coming out –"

Naima held her hand up, "Just stop ok. Where is Namiyah?" No sooner had the words left her mouth, did she hear sirens out front. Her eyes widened in horror, "You called the police already? You are just letting them take my child without knowing what's going on first?" Naima felt betrayed, now she couldn't trust her own mother. Abruptly turning to walk as quickly as she could through the house, she tried her best to locate Namiyah. There was no sign of her anywhere. The four other kids were playing in the basement as if all was right in the world. She headed up the stairs and was met by a forlorn Kaden.

"It's true isn't it?" she asked him without going up to see for herself. "Emeri's dead isn't she?"

"Yes."

"Momma thinks it was Namiyah. The police are entering as we speak."

"Well, where is she?"

Naima shrugged with tears in her eyes, "I don't know, probably somewhere running scared. I don't think she did it. I don't care what my mother says." Tears ran down her face and all Kaden could do was pull her into his arms and hold her close as the police and detectives began making their way up their stairs.

"Can you folks please follow us downstairs?" One of the officers asked.

"Sure." Kaden responded since Naima was past the point of any verbal communication at that moment.

Watching as they wheeled Emeri's body out with a while sheet over her, Naima was horrified. Her crazy, deranged half sister was dead, Namiyah was nowhere to be found, her Dad had recently passed away, Chris had killed Haven, Damir had committed suicide, and on top of all that, now she couldn't trust her own mother. Where was the world she was used to living in? It seemed like every time Emeri surfaced, crazy stuff went down, every time. Well now, she wouldn't be resurfacing would she?

Kaden could tell that Naima was at a total loss for what to do. He had never seen her so frazzled in all his life and where the hell was Namiyah? Hard to prove your innocence if you're not here to defend yourself and on the run.

"Can any of you folks tell me what happened here today?"

"I sure can, I walked in on my granddaughter exiting the

bathroom with a machete in hand. When I looked behind her, I saw Emeri's body lying there."

Naima turned to her mother and narrowed her eyes. She could not believe that her own mother would give up on her grandbaby so easily.

"Officer, there is no guarantee Namiyah did this. My mother didn't actually see or hear her do anything. She just saw her coming out of the bathroom."

"Well Ma'am, where is the girl?" One of the officers asked.

"We're not entirely sure. She ran off before you arrived."

"So we have a run away on our hands and a potential murder suspect."

"My child is not a murder suspect. What happened to innocent 'till proven guilty?" Naima yelled, "What in the hell is going on here? Momma you have lost your mind if you think I'm going to stand for this! Because of you Namiyah is somewhere running scared."

"Ma'am, please calm down. Do you have a recent photo of your daughter so we can issue an Amber Alert? We have to make it our priority to find her as soon as possible."

"I have one in my purse form when she took school pictures this year."

"Good, we'll take that and have it broadcast on all the major networks within minutes. Hopefully we should be able to pick her up by the end of the night."

Giving the officer the photo of Namiyah, Naima turned into Kaden's waiting arms. Smoothing her hair gently with his hand, Kaden didn't know what to think. In his heart, he didn't believe Namiyah was capable of murdering anyone, even her most loathed Aunt, but the circumstantial evidence against her was very incriminating. Instead of staying to fight her battle, as was her norm, she had run and no matter how he tried to twist and turn it, running screamed of guilt, because running wasn't Namiyah's style.

With his wife crying in his arms, Kaden had never felt so defenseless in his life; this was a situation that he could not control there was absolutely nothing he could do but wait it out with everyone else.

"What are we going to do?" Naima said into his chest.

Looking down into liquid hazel eyes, he responded, "I have no idea. We have to cooperate with the authorities, which mean we'll have to wait and see what happens."

"But our baby girl is out there all alone. Who knows what kind of crazies exist in the world."

"Mocha, you can't think like that. You have to hope for the best."

Wiping her face on his shirt, "There is no best and we need to leave this house. I cannot be somewhere where my child has already been tried and convicted, as she has been in this place. Let's grab the kids and go home. The police can update us from there, but I cannot stand to be around my mother for a moment longer."

"Ok Baby, anything you want. I'll get the kids and pack up all their stuff, you can wait in the car."

After Naima and Kaden left with the children; even though Cynthia's house was filled with police, she went into the basement to Kenneth's liquor cabinet and had her first drink in life.

Gagging a little on the potent liquor, she was ashamed of herself and her actions today. Naima had been right, she hadn't given Namiyah a chance to explain herself. Cynthia knew now that because of that she and Naima's relationship would never be the same.

When Cynthia had seen Namiyah standing there in front of Emeri's lifeless body with one of Kenneth's old machete's in hand, something inside of her had snapped. She had gone off on a tangent.

Grabbing the bottle of whiskey that she had taken out, Cynthia poured herself another glass. Tears began a slow steady decent down her face. She wasn't prone to crying, but lately tears were always sitting right below the surface. Life had thrown this family so many fast hard curve balls lately; even she didn't know how to handle this situation. Now because of her poor decision making her granddaughter was on the run. Cynthia prayed that Naima would be ok.

Finishing off the rest of the whiskey, Cynthia went upstairs to Emeri's room. It was a mess, someone had taken great care to make sure everything in the room was practically destroyed.

Sighing as she began the process of trying to sort through the chaotic mess, she surprisingly felt no particular way about Emeri's death. She wasn't sad, hurt or angry. She just was.

Cynthia found it hard to believe that Emeri had only been in their lives for a little over five years and no matter how she tried to work with that child; Emeri was always dead set on doing the wrong thing.

Reaching under the bed to pull everything out, Cynthia was shocked to see a book about creative ways to start a fire. "Why would Emeri have a book about starting fires?" Cynthia thought, unless, she gasped out loud, Emeri was the one responsible for Kenneth and Camille's death. So, Coleen had been right the day of Kenneth's funeral after all.

Namiyah had no idea where she was going. She just knew that she had to get away from Gram's house before the police arrived. She didn't know her Gram anymore, that lady back at the house had to have been an imposter, because her Gram would have never been so cold to her and treated her that way. Granted she had gone to Emeri's room with the intent to harm her, but someone had beaten her to the punch. Now her Gram's wanted her to pay for a crime that she didn't commit.

With no money, she didn't know what to do. She knew her mom was probably worried sick about her and searching for her, but there was no way she could go back, not while Gram's was trying to send her to jail.

Taking to the highway, she thought about hitchhiking, but quickly chose not to do that. She was aware of too many stories where hitchhikers' bodies turned up on the side of the road, or they ended up missing entirely never to be seen or heard from again.

Namiyah wondered how long she could survive without food and water. With no warning, tears began to streak down her face. This was not the way she had planned for things to go. She wasn't supposed to lose her home life and all her friends; it's a good thing Emeri was already dead, because if she wasn't Namiyah would be tempted to kill her now. Life hadn't been the same since she appeared in it and it wouldn't be the same now that she was out of it.

Looking up, Namiyah cracked her first smile of the afternoon; up the road she could see a sign for Walmart. She would be able to find some clothes and food that she could stash until she figured out what she was going to do. Sending up a salute to the sky, she said good-bye to the girl everyone knew as Namiyah. Miyah had a nice ring to it; she would use that instead, so she could keep part of herself and still not, out with the old, in with the new.

Epilogue

Gazing at Namiyah's picture with tears in her eyes, Naima couldn't believe that today was the one year anniversary of Emeri being killed and Namiyah going missing. She missed her baby girl so much. The authorities still had her listed as a missing person, but she was also a fugitive, they had went ahead and decide to charge her with murder in the first degree as well.

Shaking her head, she could not wrap her brain around so many things. She and her mother's relationship had deteriorated, as much as she wanted to, she could not forgive her for accusing Namiyah without hearing her side of the story first. "She scared my poor baby," Naima thought, "that's why she ran." To this day she still believed in Namiyah's innocence and believed that she was still alive. God had not told her otherwise, so she knew Namiyah was out there somewhere and one day she and her baby girl would be reunited.

Miyah could see her looking at the photo frame and crying. Her mother didn't know she stopped by every once in a while to check on her family. What she would give to go in and hug her mom. It had been a full year since she had been able to talk to her and hear her voice, touch her. She felt the tears and gently brushed them to the side. She knew she couldn't go home until she proved her innocence. "One day soon Mommy, I promise." She said softly before disappearing into the darkness.

ABOUT THE AUTHOR

Mychea is also the author of Coveted. She is a native of the Metropolitan of Washington, DC and is currently at work on her next novel. You can learn more about the author and future projects at www.mycheawrites.com.